Apple Is My Sign

Apple Is My Sign

by Mary Riskind

HOUGHTON MIFFLIN COMPANY
BOSTON

Library of Congress Cataloging in Publication Data
Riskind, Mary.
  Apple is my sign.
  SUMMARY: A 10-year-old boy returns to his parents'
apple farm for the holidays after his first term at a school
for the deaf in Philadelphia.
  [1. Deaf—Fiction. 2. Physically handicapped—Fiction]
I. Title.
PZ7.R493Ap   [Fic]   80-39746
HC ISBN 0-395-30852-6   PA ISBN 0-395-65747-4

Printed in the United States of America
AGM   10 9 8 7 6 5 4 3

In memory of my father, Harry,
and for Mom, Paul, and Steve
with much love

Contents

Author's Note

I am a hearing person, but I grew up in a family with deaf parents. I learned to talk with my hands before I learned to talk with my voice. The characters in this book are deaf, like my mother and father, and they are using sign language, just as we did at home. As you read this book, you will find that what Apple Harry and his friends say to each other is not like everyday speech. One of the problems I discovered in writing about deaf children is that it is hard to translate sign language into English, so I would like to tell you a little bit about how I have done that here.

One of the things you will notice is that words in the dialogue sometimes are spelled out, or finger-spelled. In the manual alphabet each letter is represented by a particular hand-shape. Some of them look like the written letter: *O* and *C* are examples. But the letter *S* is made by a fist. You can say anything you want with the manual alphabet, but people usually fingerspell only at certain times: if there is no sign for a word; to say the proper name of a person or place, such as a city (although there are a few common signs for big cities like Chicago and Washington, D.C.); or to give emphasis to a word — a little like raising your voice.

Deaf people typically use some combination of signs and fingerspelling. A person who speaks sign language well can go as fast as (even faster than) you can say the same things out loud. Signs are what make it possible to go so fast.

There are different kinds of signs. Some signs act out, or pantomime, the ideas they are supposed to represent. Hold your first two fingers over your ear and wiggle them backward. Does that make you think of rabbit ears? You have just said the word *rabbit*. Some signs do not look at all like what they mean but they belong to groups of signs all made in a similar way. Let me give you an example. Signs that have to do with being female (*mother, sister, daughter, aunt, girl*) are all made by touching the lower half of the face. Male signs are made by touching the upper half of the face.

Some signs are initializations, made by shaking the first letter of the word, such as *g* for *green*. There are also signs deaf people learn, depending on where they grew up or go to school. For instance, I've noticed that people from different areas use a different sign for *candy*.

How you say a sign is important. Signs can change meaning if they are repeated, or if they are said slower or faster, or if you point the sign away from or toward yourself. You turn your hand away to say 'catch-him' and toward yourself to say 'catch-me.' Your facial expression is also part of making a sign. It should match the sign. If you frown as you form the sign for *pleased* or *happy*, a deaf person would find you difficult to understand.

Sign language is very condensed, or telegraphic. Oftentimes word endings (*-s, -ly, -ed, -ing*) and little words (*is, am, are, has, had, I, the*) are omitted, and a single sign will do the work of two or more English words to communicate an idea. In the dialogue you will also see many hyphenated words, like 'thank-you' and 'show-me.' These are words said by a single sign.

Word order in sign language often is not the same as its English translation. 'See before that finish' said in sign becomes "I've already seen that before" in English. I wanted to give you a feeling for sign language, but without confusing you, so I stayed with

English word order through most of the story, and sometimes I added little words or endings.

Sign language is changing today. My parents learned sign and they taught it to me the way Apple Harry speaks. But to help younger deaf people learn English more easily new signs are being developed and introduced. For example, there are now signs for the words *is, am,* and *are,* and their use is spreading.

I hope you enjoy getting to know Apple Harry. If you would like to know more about deaf people and sign language, please write to the

> National Association of the Deaf
> 814 Thayer Avenue
> Silver Spring, Maryland 20910

Mary Riskind

Chapter 1

Mail Call

Harry picked at his plate of apple fritters and scrapple. With the knot deep in his stomach he just didn't feel hungry.

Up and down the table hands flew. Some boys visited across the table, or side by side, and one conversation leapfrogged over another. Harry followed the discussion at the far end uninvited. A large-eared boy wearing spectacles was telling a story about someone signed 'Rapid Heart.' Harry wasn't certain, but he thought 'Rapid Heart' was Mr. Thomas, their proctor. His sign was the letter T tapped against the chest, but Harry often noticed the boys using this second sign.

Another fellow with dimples set deep into his heavy

cheeks ambled over to the table and joined the conversation. The rest called him 'Mighty.'

Harry glumly stabbed a fritter. He didn't even understand their names. A few were obvious — like the boy with the wire-rim glasses. His name looked like two round circles over the eyes. Or the one beside him who went by 'Cowlick' for the yellow hair standing in a haystack above his forehead. But what about the boy who was signed by a tug on the right ear? Or 'Mighty'? And what about 'Rapid Heart'?

Spectacles pushed away from the table. He was hurrying the others to mail call. This was the moment Harry had dreaded all morning. He trailed behind the boys down the corridor from the dining hall to the high-ceilinged foyer and took a position outside the circle.

Their proctor, mustached, not yet crumpled by the day, appeared and lifted a mail pouch over their heads. The boys clawed like puppies.

On the opposite side of the foyer near the girls' stairs, a slender erect woman carried a second pouch. The girls bunched around her. Harry thought of his sisters. He missed Veve and Anna. Here — in the dining room, in study hall, in morning classes — the girls always were in another part of the room. Maybe it was like this in a hearing school. They never joined the boys' games and the boys never ventured up the girls' stairs. He wondered what they did there.

Mr. Thomas peered at a letter from the bag. His hands waved. Harry studied each gesture. 'B-r-o-w-n,' he announced, then finished with a snagging motion, as if pulling in a fish.

A boy in a blue flannel shirt stepped forward. He stuffed his envelope inside his cap without reading it. It was considered bad manners here to read mail under everyone's noses, but Harry saw them — during classes or over lunch — devouring their letters like stolen sweets. He hoped for a turn, too, for a letter saying he could go home. He'd hoped for more than two weeks already.

Mr. Thomas turned the pouch upside-down and shook it. Empty again.

Harry bit his tongue to fight the brimming tears and ran out the front door of the school and down the steps. His foot missed the bottom step and he stumbled, almost falling.

When he reached the end of the driveway, he poked his head through the iron bars of the gate. Outside, a maple tossed her scarlet headdress and a golden-haired elm bowed. On the farm he loved the fall, when trees wakened from their green sleep and spoke to him in noisy orange and yellow tongues, as surely as if he could hear.

He turned from the trees and watched a horse-drawn trolley stop at the corner. Two people, a man and a woman, stepped down. He recognized the woman. She was the one who scowled whenever he went back for seconds on rolls or dessert. They disappeared around the corner in the direction of the back entrance.

He squeezed his eyes and squeezed the rails. If only the gate would swing free.

Someone tugged his shoulder from behind, startling him. He didn't bother to see whose it was. He hit the hand away hard.

The hand was Mighty's. Up close he looked older than Harry's big brother Ray — maybe even twelve — and he stood at least a head taller. Harry glowered and braced himself for a shove. The boy stared, then handed over a small package. Harry's heart leapt. He recognized his father's handwriting.

The boy wheeled and headed up the walkway. 'Come,' he motioned. Harry lagged a few paces behind. But the slower he walked the slower the other boy walked. Finally the boy stopped and waited for him. His hands fluttered. 'New to school here?' he asked.

'Yes,' Harry answered.

'I here — soon four years,' the boy said. 'First not like. After-while you like. Work, work, but good fun, fooling, play tease. My name L——.' He formed the letter L and rotated it over his stomach. 'Short for L-a-n-d-i-s,' he fingerspelled. 'What your name?'

'H-a-r-r-y.' Harry paused. 'I thought saw boys name you Mighty.'

'My second sign. Not necessary call me Mighty. I like L—— better. You have sign?' Landis asked.

Harry flushed. 'Apple.' He hastened to explain. 'Older brother give-me name. Because while young always pick-up apples. Father has apple farm. Keep many, many apples in my pockets. Sometimes with worms. Not care. Love play, play with apples.'

'Good name,' said Landis. 'Home call me Baby. Once someone from school saw. Boys make fun. Make me very angry. We fight. I winner. Now name me Mighty.'

'Now understand.' Harry's fist circled his chest, then he extended his hand, palm out. 'Sorry push. Thank-you for bringing this.' Landis nodded.

They reached the school building. Mr. Thomas was waiting in the entranceway. 'Why skip-off?' he demanded.

Harry didn't answer. He pointed to his package. 'Let-me carry to sleep-room?'

'Yes. Go-on. Hurry.'

Harry cleared the wide wood stairs two at a time and dashed for the row of neatly made beds nearest the windows. Mrs. Slack glanced up from her folding and sorting in the laundry adjoining the dormitory room.

Mrs. Slack was like her pair of heavy black shoes, sturdy and strict. The first week of school she had rubbed a boy's mouth with soap for not paying attention when she showed them how to make their beds. Later that day Harry had taken a small taste of the yellow soap — the tiniest bite — and knew he didn't ever want her angry with him.

'Why here?' Her face furrowed as she mouthed the hearing words and signed at the same time. Harry showed her the package. She went back to her work without asking anything more. He breathed a sigh of relief.

He reached under the bed for his footlocker and opened the lid so Mrs. Slack wouldn't see. His hands were trembling a little. He removed the string, carefully wound it, and put it in a pocket to save. He smoothed the brown wrapping and tucked it inside his locker. Then he spread the contents before him: two drawing pencils, a thin pocket knife on a fine chain, a soft charcoal eraser, a packet of new cream-colored paper, and a letter.

He turned the letter many times without opening it. Finally, he unfolded the page. The script was clear and flowing.

September 29, 1899

My dearest son Harry,

I enclose a small present from Mother and me. We hope these will help you feel happy at school. If you have time, Ray would like a drawing of school and of your friends.

We did not send you to Philadelphia because we think you are more trouble. I always dreamed of going to school. It is too late for me. Now I dream of schooling for you. You are better suited for school than Ray, and your sisters are too young. Ray does not love books. He will be a farmer like me.

In town there are only the hearing and their children. At Mr. Bertie's school you will meet people who are like us, you will learn a trade, and maybe some day you will help other deaf.

I know you are homesick. I talked again with Preacher Ervin, and he tells you to be patient. Soon you will make friends, have good times, and forget your troubles.

I think of you often and cross my fingers for you to be happy.

> *Your loving father,*
> *Harry Berger*

Harry crumpled the letter. The hearing again. His father only wanted him away from the hearing. Didn't he know they were everywhere? Even at Mr. Bertie's?

He was so suspicious of them, expecting the shop-keepers in town to shortchange him, or blaming the friends Harry made there for anything he did wrong.

Right up to the day he left for school, Harry had been teaching one of the boys from Muncy sign language — like Preacher Ervin — hoping that would change his father's mind. Freckles stood on the platform and fingerspelled 'G-o-o-d-b-y-e.' But Harry's father took no notice. Nothing could crack that granite stare, not when his mind was set.

Harry wadded the letter into a tight ball and threw it. He wanted to go home! He wanted to climb the apple trees. He wanted to bite into a sun-warmed apple and taste the burst of sweet wet. And he wanted to run — going and going until he dropped breathless. He was tired of sitting at desks, standing in lines to brush his teeth, lines to get his food, and tired of grownups forever telling him to hurry.

The tears he'd held in check for days welled up and spilled over.

Something moved in the doorway. Landis. He waved. 'Come. Late. Mr. Thomas looking.'

Harry quickly wiped his face and stashed his presents under his pillow. Before Landis could ask questions, he ran past him to the boys' toilet room. 'T-T-T.'

Chapter 2

Pictures

After dinner Harry unpacked a pair of trousers and a couple of shirts from his locker and hung them on the hooks above his bed — he guessed he'd need them now that he was staying — and he collected his charcoal pencils and paper to take with him to study hour.

Landis took a seat across from him at the table and nodded a greeting. Harry's head bobbed shyly.

He rolled the pencils between his fingers. They were smooth, well-balanced, better than the ones he usually had. His father must have been eager to please him. He folded and unfolded the knife. He whittled the end of one of the pencils to a fine point, and played with the shavings until they crumbled and scattered. Then he huddled over a sheet of the paper.

He rubbed the charcoal in short, even strokes. Soon the form of a building emerged, then out of that two long arms and a wide brick portico with stairs that swept around either side and met in front. A cobble-stone walkway extended from the building through the trees to a high brick fence and iron gate. He penciled in the sign he remembered hanging in the front: THE BERTIE SCHOOL FOR THE DEAF.

Landis reached over for his attention. 'Jealous,' he said. 'You draw very good.' He made his signs small to escape the study proctor's notice.

Harry felt his ears burn. 'For my brother. Never saw school.'

'Can you draw something for me?'

'Maybe. What?'

'Anything. Think idea yourself.'

Harry hesitated. 'Will try.' He started once, discarded the paper, started again and discarded that piece, too. Suddenly he fell to work. When he was finished he kicked Landis's foot, then passed his picture under the table.

Landis examined the drawing in his lap. His face broke into a smirk. Landis gave the picture to his neighbor on the right and fingerspelled 'H-a-r-r-y.' The boy looked over, winked his approval, and passed it to the person next to him, and so on, until the paper traveled full circle round the table.

All of a sudden the study proctor swooped beside Landis and ripped the drawing out of his hands. 'Whose? Yours?' All eyes in the long room turned.

Landis declined to say anything. The rest sat rigid.

The proctor spied Harry's pencils and the small sheaf of paper. 'Yours.' She pursed her lips as if she'd tasted something bitter, and stabbed a finger at the sketch. It was an outrageous caricature of Mr. Thomas with a great walrus mustache and heart-shaped head. 'Study. Not play.' She scooped up the drawing materials and returned with them to her desk.

Harry looked desperately to Landis.

'Not worry,' Landis said. 'Lady not cross.'

Harry was not persuaded. He was miserable.

Moments later Landis poked him. 'Watch-me,' he said with a toothy grin. He reached beneath the table. His hand reappeared blackened with boot polish. He rubbed his chubby left cheek, leaving a dark sooty mark. Harry watched, mystified.

Landis tapped Spectacles, who was sitting to his left, with his elbow. 'My face dirty?' he asked. Spectacles — one eye on Landis, one on the proctor — nodded his head yes and buried his nose in his book.

Then Landis tapped the person on his right side and repeated the question, pointing to his right cheek. 'No,' the boy on the right said.

'But he says my face dirty.' Landis pointed to Spectacles. The right-hand fellow inspected Landis's face again and shook his head no.

Landis turned to his left once more. 'Hey,' he nudged Spectacles, 'he says my face clean.' Landis looked right and left. 'Who right?' Hands on either side of Landis flared.

'Wrong!'

'You blind.'

'You stupid.'

'Who stupid? You stupid!'

Finally, Landis raised his hands as though to calm the unruly mob. 'Look.' He displayed first his left cheek to the boy on the right, then his right cheek to the left. Landis leaned back in his chair and rested his hands on his plump belly. He smiled from ear to ear.

'Wait.' Spectacles waved a warning toward the proctor, who was showing too much interest in their table. 'I will catch-you. You see,' he threatened.

'H-a, h-a, h-a,' Landis jeered.

The hour was finished. Landis and Harry walked together to the proctor's desk. 'New boy?' the proctor asked. 'Drawings very good.' She handed over Harry's art supplies but held back the pictures of Mr. Thomas and of the school. 'I keep pictures. Want show. What your name?'

'H-a-r-r-y B-e-r-g-e-r.' Harry's heart pounded. 'Pictures for brother.'

'Will give-back later.' She packed up her belongings, including the pictures. There was nothing for Harry to do but leave.

'Bad happen. Maybe make trouble for me because o-f pictures,' Harry said to Landis, as they walked to the dormitory.

'Nothing bad happen,' Landis said. 'Big heart, same father. That B-e-r-t-i-e's daughter. Better forget.' They proceeded a bit farther; then Landis stopped. 'You never tell-me. How-old you?' he asked. 'Me twelve.'

Harry smiled. He'd guessed right. 'Ten.'

'Ten? Short, whew. Think eight, eight. Maybe seven!'

'Short, all my family.'

'Good you have sign. Maybe boys hang name Short.'

Harry shrugged off this last comment. 'Not care,' he lied.

'Where your home?'

'Farm near M-u-n-c-y, P-a. Where yours?'

Landis shook the letter P. 'Philadelphia. Here.'

'Good for you. Easy go home,' Harry answered.

'Maybe. Like school better. Home, only-one deaf. Small fun.'

'Your mother, father talking?'

'Yes.'

Harry was surprised. 'Both?' Sitting at the school dinner table he usually knew which children came from hearing families, especially the younger ones. Their hands were stilted, harder to understand. He liked this boy's signs. They were large and friendly. 'Brother, sister deaf?' Harry asked.

'No brother, sister.'

'Who teach-you sign-language?'

'Visiting preacher. Name E-r-v-i-n. During small.'

'I know preacher! I know, I know! Can hear? Yes. That same man who tell mother, father about deaf school.' Harry was elated that they might know the same person. 'Before, teach here. Now preach-around, around P-a farms. Bring news from all ears closed.' He extended the sign for 'all' to show how large the scope of Mr. Ervin's travels was.

'Yes, yes,' Landis nodded, 'same man.'

'Beautiful signs,' Harry said. 'My father not like hearing, but welcome E-r-v-i-n. I think because preacher sign good. Look same deaf.'

'E-r-v-i-n mother, father deaf.'

'Not-know before.' Harry's hands stopped. No wonder Preacher Ervin signed so comfortably. 'How you deaf?' he asked Landis.

'Sick. S-c-a-r-l-e-t f-e-v-e-r. Three years-old. Lose hearing. You?'

'Born deaf. Mother, father, all deaf.'

'Easy for you.'

Harry did not understand.

'You not lonely,' Landis explained. 'My mother, father not like signing. First want me talk. Read-lips.'
Landis's face broke into a perfect imitation of the big,
chewing mouths the hearing people who worked about
the school used to make the children understand.

Harry laughed and laughed. It felt so good to laugh.
Then he recalled his drawings. What if Mr. Thomas
saw them? 'Why Mr. Thomas signed Rapid Heart?'
he asked when the laughter slowed.

'You not know?' Landis's eyes widened and his gestures grew excited. 'Mr. Thomas engaged B-e-r-t-i-e
daughter.'

'Lady who take my pictures?' Harry's hand went to
his mouth.

'Yes! That one.' Landis mimicked her stiff-necked
gait. 'Once boys find Mr. Thomas and daughter. Kiss,
kiss, kiss behind stairs. They think covered. He see
us — face red. Now we name-him Rapid Heart.'

Harry puckered his lips, made the sign of a wildly
beating heart, and swooned to the floor, rolling his
eyes heavenward.

'Yes. Yes. Perfect right,' Landis rejoiced. He doubled over and tumbled onto the floor beside Harry.
The two boys lay there giggling.

Harry's sides were aching when they made their
way at last to the sleeping room. As they stepped
through the doorway, they saw Spectacles and several

of the other boys arrayed along the opposite wall. A flurry of soft objects rushed toward them. It was raining pillows, blankets, bathrobes, and towels.

Landis picked up a pillow and whacked the person nearest him over the head. 'Not me,' the boy protested. 'One watch.'

Harry grabbed a blanket and swung it in a whirlwind around his head.

They were pelted with more pillows. Landis and Harry ran from bed to bed, heaving back whatever they could lay their hands on, and from corner to corner searching for a defensible position.

They were standing on a bed when Harry ducked under a pillow and fell into Landis. The two of them collapsed, exhausted with fun. The other boys swarmed over them, tickling and roughhousing until Landis pleaded for mercy.

Spectacles stood over them. 'See?' he boasted, 'I told-you.'

After the gas lamps were turned down, Harry slipped out of bed and felt his way in the black night to Landis's bed. Harry fingerspelled, 'Y-o-u t-h-i-n-k B-e-r-t-i-e s-e-n-d m-e h-o-m-e f-o-r p-i-c-t-u-r-e-s.' He drew a question mark on Landis's palm.

Landis touched his hand. 'N-o. N-o.' His hands were big and comforting. Harry made his way back to bed and slept soundly.

Chapter 3

"Singer"

For the next few days Harry made it a practice to bury himself in the thick of the lunchroom crowd or any line, and Landis delivered his mail. He hoped if Mr. Thomas didn't see him he'd forget to be angry about the picture.

In time he'd nearly forgotten the drawing himself, so it came as a rude jolt one afternoon when Mr. Thomas strode directly to him in the print shop. 'Come,' he motioned and led the way to the corridor. Harry's stomach fluttered.

'B-e-r-t-i-e want see-you,' Mr. Thomas said. The flutter turned to cold fear.

Mr. Thomas accompanied him to the headmaster's

office, ushered him to the overstuffed chair opposite Mr. Bertie, then gazed out the window.

Mr. Bertie reached in a drawer and placed two sheets of paper on the desk blotter. There were his drawings. The bloated walrus-face lay on top. He stiffened.

'Drawing perfect,' Mr. Bertie flourished. 'You like draw?'

'Yes. Since little,' Harry signed weakly.

'Who teach-you?'

'Mother. And myself,' he answered, confused. These weren't the kinds of questions he expected.

'Want learn more?'

Now he was truly confused. He didn't know what to say. Mr. Bertie repeated his question. Hesitant, he nodded yes.

Mr. Bertie leaned over his desk. 'Wonder maybe you change. No-more printing. Go to t-a-i-l-o-r-i-n-g. Study clothing design. Study much more drawing. Cutting. Sewing. Think you like?'

Harry began to relax. What he'd learned in the print shop so far was tedious, though he enjoyed reading the finished copy.

'Well?' Mr. Bertie prodded.

He didn't know about tailoring, except his mother did do mending and sewing for townspeople in

Muncy. On the other hand, he knew he loved draw-ing. 'Try?' Harry said.

The elderly man beamed. 'Fine. Settled. Mr. Thomas lead-you now.' He spoke a few words to Mr. Thomas, then he rose and handed over the sketch of the school to Harry. He held on to the other one. 'Allow-me keep this? Face very funny.'

Harry looked to Mr. Thomas, who had stopped be-fore the coat-closet mirror. He was giving the tips of his mustache a satisfied twist. Mr. Bertie winked at Harry.

Harry grinned.

When Harry arrived at the textile room, he was surprised to see mostly girls — there were none in the print shop — and a handful of the older boys, who he knew slept in the third-floor dormitory. A few people paused from their work and smiled or gestured hello.

A short, quick man wearing a pincushion strapped to his wrist and a green visor showed him to a slant-top desk beside the windows. 'Since first day, you look, try new things. Tomorrow work. Any questions, ask — ' He fingered the other pupils watching their exchange. 'I-f they not know, come see me.' And he was gone.

Harry hopped aboard the stool. The desk was ar-rayed with leads, pen points, holders, rulers, jars of ink, and other interesting items he didn't recognize. He reached first for a wood figurine. To his surprise it was flexible. The arms, the knees, the torso, bent. He twisted the form into a series of improbable positions — legs wrapped around the neck, crawling on all fours upside-down, or rolled into a ball.

A curly head grinned at him above the top of his board. The girl caught his eye. 'Silly,' he remarked, referring to the wood doll. 'What for?'

'Copy. Move any, how you want, then copy,' she said. 'Paper in drawer. Down right.'

In the drawer he found several kinds: heavy coarse sheets, satin smooth sheets, and thin translucent skins. He selected a pen point and holder and a piece of the heavy paper. After fumbling with the point, he finally jammed it into the cork handle. He was opening a jar of ink when the curly head peered over again.

'Shake first,' she said.

He shook. Black ink slopped out the sides and spattered on his fresh sheet of paper.

The girl laughed. 'No. No. Push-down-top first. Then shake. Better smooth paper for i-n-k. Rough good for black pencil,' she lectured.

Harry mopped up with a handkerchief. He was starting to feel irked with this know-it-all girl. He pointedly flipped the coarse paper clean side up and slid the edges under two thin slats hinged to the board. He wondered if she'd noticed he figured out how to hold the papers without her.

Then the pen dragged and ink oozed outward. The line he drew spread into a blotch. Phooey! The print shop was never like this.

The instructor stopped at Harry's table. 'Mistake.' He reached in the drawer and pulled out a smoother, harder sheet of paper. 'Best for i-n-k.' He whisked past.

Harry hunched down low, keeping his paper out of view of the curly-headed girl. He made a tiny mark with his pen. The ink behaved and stayed in its place. This was better. He unwound the figurine and molded it to resemble a person running; he sketched a front view first, then a side view.

'Good. Good. Perfect.' The instructor was at his side again. Harry sat a little straighter. The teacher gestured to the other side of his drawing board. 'A-g-n-e-s, show new boy sewing machine. And materials.' Agnes obediently climbed off her stool to stand next to him.

Agnes, Harry thought. His mother had an aunt named Agnes. He liked her pictures but he didn't like this Agnes.

Agnes stole a look at Harry's drawings. 'Nice,' she said. Harry scowled.

When Agnes led the way to the cutting tables, Harry loitered as far back as he could. The tables were

APPLE IS MY SIGN

heaped with fabrics. Agnes handed Harry several scraps. The material was soft, yet tightly woven and strong. It was finer than anything he had seen before.

'Man's coat, pants,' Agnes explained, 'for rich.' She extended the sign for 'rich' to suggest an awesome stack of money. It wasn't easy, but Harry managed not to smile.

Next she showed him to an empty machine. Ornate gold letters spelled out "Singer" across a black metal arm. Singer, he remarked to himself. Why Singer?

Agnes spun the wheel with her right hand. She pedaled the treadle and guided two pieces of material under the needle. 'Careful fingers. I-f needle in. Ouch.'

She halted a moment and reached for his hand. He pulled it away. She looked angry. 'Mule. Want show something.' He yielded reluctantly. She placed his hand on the sewing machine, then resumed her stitching. The machine hummed into his fingertips with the light rumble of a satisfied cat under his hand. He smiled in spite of himself.

'Now me,' he begged. Agnes moved over on the bench.

The machine spun a couple of times, then stopped abruptly. 'What wrong?' he asked.

'Feet.' Agnes showed him how to keep his feet in rhythm with the wheel.

He made one or two false starts, but at last he had

it. His feet rocked back and forth, back and forth, while the Singer purred. They took turns working the treadle the remainder of the afternoon and Harry listened with his fingers.

'Feel wonderful! Feel wonderful!' he said. 'Now I understand why named Sing e-r.' He repeated the sign for 'sing,' waving his arm as he'd seen the choir director do at Mr. Bertie's hearing church. Singer. It was the perfect name. Agnes wasn't bad either.

Chapter 4

Brotherhood

Two days later, at lunch hour, Agnes motioned to Harry from the girls' side of the dining room. 'Walk together?' she asked. 'Something tell-you.' Harry felt all eyes at his table watching him. He nodded quickly and returned to his meal.

Lunch was nearly finished when he felt his plate shake. Cowlick was rapping on the table beside him. 'Hey, Apple. Girl want talk-to you.'

Now what could she want? Harry turned and looked over. But Agnes was busy talking to the girl beside her.

The boys laughed. 'Like girl. Apple like girl,' Cowlick teased. Cowlick petted and caressed his hand, and soon every other boy at the table was swooning.

Harry's face burned. He squeezed his eyes shut and refused to see anything further Cowlick had to say.

On their way to class Agnes had a story about their tailoring teacher, Mr. Wing. Yesterday one of the girls found his visor on a desk and left it in plain sight hanging on a dressmaking form. Agnes's head stooped. 'Wing where, where. Cap still on maybe.' When Harry didn't laugh, she looked disappointed. For all that humiliation, he thought, her story wasn't even funny.

The whole afternoon Harry jumped from one drawing to the next. He couldn't complete any of them. All he could think about was how to even the score with Cowlick.

As soon as they finished in the textile shop, he raced to the football field, where the upper-form team was already scrimmaging. They had an important game coming, this time with a hearing school.

Harry paced, waiting. Football was new to him since he came to Mr. Bertie's, but he'd thrown himself into the game from the first day. By now he played as well as any of them, including Cowlick.

The boys arrived in twos and threes. Finally there were enough of them to move to an adjacent field and choose up sides. Landis appointed himself captain of one team, and before Harry had a chance Spectacles pushed himself forward to be the second captain.

Landis chose first. 'Apple.' Harry stepped forward and stood beside Landis.

Spectacles tugged his ear. Now James left the clump of boys.

Landis conferred with Harry. 'Which you think? Ralph or Cowlick?'

'No, no. Not Cowlick.'

'Why not? Good player.'

'My business. You see,' Harry said.

Landis hesitated briefly, then motioned for Ralph. On the next round Spectacles waved to Cowlick. Harry was pleased. He'd wanted him to be on the opposing team.

In the huddle Harry signaled, 'Cowlick mine. No one touch. One me.' The others looked to Landis.

'Why?' Landis challenged him.

'My reason.'

'No good. Must tell-me first.'

'Not want.'

'Cowlick tall than you. I-f only you follow, maybe lose.'

'I can beat.' Harry was fuming now. 'Cowlick think smart. Make fun on me. I show-him who smart. Must revenge.'

'O-K,' Landis said. He signed to the others. 'All agree?' They nodded their heads.

The ball moved. Cowlick ran to the side. Harry

dashed pell-mell to the same side and shoved him down as hard as he could. Next, Cowlick tackled one of their team and Harry jumped onto the struggling, squirming heap of arms and legs. Pile-up after pile-up, whenever Cowlick went down, Harry was right on top of him.

Cowlick emerged from a tackle, and when he found Harry, he pushed him aside. 'Keep-away,' he threatened with a fist.

Still Harry dogged him and his dogging was taking its toll. Cowlick was tiring. Once he almost lost the ball. Another time he took too long to decide where to run and Harry dropped him near the starting line.

All too soon it was time to go inside and wash up for supper. Harry almost didn't care whose team was winning; he was so intent on Cowlick. And he wasn't finished with him yet. He motioned. 'Hey, Cowlick. You slow. Same cow.' He worked his mouth chewing his cud. Cowlick turned in the other direction.

All through dinner and study hall whenever Cowlick happened to look Harry's way, Harry chewed and chewed.

They were returning to the dormitory room when Cowlick issued his challenge. 'Fight?'

'Yes!' Harry was eager.

The boys lined up on either wall of the dormitory room like two opposing armies. Cowlick heaved the first pillow, the signal for the others to start. Harry returned fire.

A pillow landed at Harry's feet. He grabbed and hurled. His aim was good. Then Harry saw what he'd thrown.

The pillow was not a pillow. It was a slipper, heading straight for Cowlick's face. Harry waved, 'Watch! S-l-i-p —' Too late. The heel of the slipper caught Cowlick in the eye. The battle was over almost before it started.

Cowlick cried. Harry rushed to him. 'Sorry, sorry, sorry.' He bent to look. Harry sucked in a sharp breath and shook his right hand slowly. Within minutes Cowlick's eye was swollen shut, the right side of his face a tender purple. Harry felt wretched.

Someone sent for Mrs. Slack and she sent for Mr. Thomas. 'Who responsible?' Mr. Thomas demanded.

Harry was about to step forward and confess when Landis shot Harry a discouraging headshake, no.

'No one fault,' Cowlick answered Mr. Thomas. 'Playing. A-c-c-i-d-e-n-t.'

'Bad hurt eye. Someone blame for. Who? Must punish,' Mr. Thomas said.

Again Harry wanted to confess, but this time it was Cowlick who plucked at his shirt sleeve, and Harry stopped.

'A-c-c-i-d-e-n-t,' Cowlick insisted.

Mr. Thomas stared at each boy in the circle with dismay. No one moved. 'No one play outside until tell-me who.' His gaze passed around the circle a second time. Still no one stirred. 'Then final. All punish.' Mr. Thomas swept from the room.

Harry sat with Cowlick and held the ice pack to his face. 'Why not tell? My fault.' Each time he looked at Cowlick's face he felt worse. He deserved to be punished, but not the others.

'I know you not mean for hurt. I first ask fight. Anyway, we all same. Important, deaf must together.' Cowlick wrapped an arm around Harry's shoulder.

The other boys standing around the bed nodded emphatically. 'Yes,' one said. 'True,' another said. 'Right. Deaf never tattle. Always together.'

A new kind of happiness surged up in Harry. It made him prickly and at the same time he almost could cry.

Over the next several days, he watched Cowlick's eye carefully. Cowlick's eyelids turned from purple to green, green to yellow, then yellow to flesh. At last he could relax.

He worked hard the following Saturday at composing his monthly 'home-letter.' That was Mr. Bertie's term; Landis and the boys called it their 'must-letter.' Most of the others were finished and skipped out early, while he was still poring over his paper. He told his parents about his love for this new game, football, about kind Mr. Bertie, about how much he enjoyed drawing classes, but somehow these things didn't really amount to why they were right to keep him at school.

He thought of his brother Ray on the farm and he was pinched with sadness for all Ray was missing. He finished:

Preacher Ervin was right. I have made friends and I am happy here at school. You can uncross your fingers.

Lovingly,
Your son Harry

He dropped his letter on the proctor's desk and ran out the hall and out the building the long way, down the majestic front steps, round the building to the playing field.

Cowlick hailed when he saw him, 'We need you. They winning.'

Chapter 5

'M-o-t-o-r-c-a-r'

Mr. Bertie was escorting his pupils to the hearing church a few blocks from school. Harry dawdled at the end of the line of bobbing caps and ribbons as he did every Sunday, and stared into homes and buildings and down the streets they left untraveled, when suddenly the column broke and swarmed by the side of the road.

Harry caught up and pushed to the center. At rest on the cobblestones was the strangest thing he had ever seen. It was a little like a carriage: open, boxy, hinges everywhere, and metal parts that angled to the

rear. But there were few places to sit and no conceiva-
ble place to hitch a horse.

The children at the outside edge jostled those in
front for a turn. Now Mr. Bertie pressed close. He
looked under the thing's wheels and patted its
lanterns.

'I know! I know! I see before, many times in Philadelphia,' Landis boasted. 'Name m-o-t-o-r-c-a-r.' The
word 'm-o-t-o-r-c-a-r' rippled through the group. The
boys crowded around Landis.

'How you know?' Ralph challenged.

'Father tell-me.'

'What for?' Harry asked.

'Wonderful! Wheels roll without horses. For riding.
Little-bit same train. Wonderful!'

Harry looked at Landis skeptically. How could it be
like a train? There were no tracks. And the thing
wasn't nearly the size of a train.

Just then a man in goggles and a handsome plaid
scarf made his way through the gathering and climbed
into the vehicle.

The headmaster flung his arms, 'Back! Back!' The
children fanned out, giving the man and his strange
carriage room. A jab here, a twist of his wrist, and the
motorcar shook violently. Again a poke, a hand on the
lever, the man doffed his cap, and the carriage was
rolling. It was rolling! Harry and a couple of other

boys chased alongside until the motorcar picked up speed and they had to drop away.

Watching after the shrinking motorcar, Mr. Bertie said, in his most florid signs, 'God truly marvelous.'

The congregation was already seated when they arrived at the church. Mr. Bertie stood in the doorway and put finger to lips, meaning quiet. It was a new concept to Harry, like football, but not like football, because in football he knew what to do. The best he could figure for quiet was it meant not to stir, so Harry moved as little as possible as he climbed to the second-floor balcony.

But the hearing people craned and ogled them anyway, and Mr. Bertie's brow wrinkled. Whatever quiet was, they weren't doing it, not right.

On the floor beneath them the congregation rose in a body, as if lifted on the minister's outstretched robes. The organist reached hand over hand for a distant part of the keyboard, while her feet bounced on pipes under the bench.

Usually the organist was Harry's favorite part of the hearing church. If her head tilted and her arms and back swayed, Harry imagined the music was sunlight glancing off a pool, and when her feet danced very fast, he fantasized a deer, or maybe a rabbit, in flight. But today he tired of the game. He felt bitten with some kind of a madness. His mind returned over and over to the motorcar like fingers to an uncontrollable itch. If motorcars roamed Philadelphia's streets, what other miracles did it hold?

Harry sought out Landis on their way back to the school. 'Tell-me more Philadelphia. See many new things? Or one m-o-t-o-r-c-a-r?'

'No. Not one. Many, many interesting things. New. New. Always new,' Landis replied. 'I love stores. Shelves, high, to ceiling. Top shelf boxes — how think bring-down?'

Harry couldn't guess.

'With long wood pole. More tall than man. True. Top, same-as hand. M-e-t-a-l. Like-this.' And Landis demonstrated pulling a lever at the bottom of an imaginary pole to open and close the pincers at the other end and in one slick maneuver releasing a tin box into an outstretched hand. Harry was awestruck.

'Not look-around Philadelphia with mother, father?' Landis asked.

'Train to school. That's-all.'

Landis looked sorry for him. 'Best fun, watch people. Most interesting.' They walked on a bit, then Landis continued. 'One time with mother, father see big b-e-l-l. Crack. Father say no good. No sound.'

'Broken?' Harry asked.

'Deaf, same us.' Landis laughed.

'Home have b-e-l-l,' Harry said. 'See often near

34

school. Wonder, wonder, what for? Think silly, need big hat, for what?' He pretended to put his head inside the big hat and, arms out, he groped and stumbled. 'Think maybe hearing large head.'

Landis grinned. 'Yes, yes.'

'Happen once,' Harry went on, 'see hearing boys fool with.' Now he yanked a rope. 'Again, again. Afterwhile boys gone. Me see. Find inside ball, hard. Surprise. Pull. Feel shake-shake.' He paused. 'Now know for shake-shake head.' Harry's body jerked. 'Shakeshake-shake.' Then the two boys took turns and one pulled as the other twitched.

'Bet your b-e-l-l stink small,' Landis said, still giggling. 'Philadelphia has large.' He flung his arms to show how enormous. 'Must for large, large head.' And he doubled over laughing again.

'Wait,' said Harry, suddenly serious. 'Very, very large? True?'

'Yes.'

Harry grew excited. 'Call L-i-b-e-r-t-y?'

'Yes, think call. Know?'

'Yes, yes. Read about. My favorite history, soldiers and war. Before read about L-i-b-e-r-t-y. Forget in Philadelphia. Don't-know, maybe think another Philadelphia place. But find here. Here,' he repeated. 'Wonderful.'

'Think funny keep b-e-l-l, broken,' Landis said.

35

'You knock-head. For history. For remember begin America. First in America.'

'Maybe broken because old.'

'No, no. New. Happen, don't-know why.' Harry reflected on the bell. 'Wish see.'

The two boys stopped where they had seen the motorcar earlier. There was no sign of it. 'How think m-o-t-o-r-c-a-r can roll without horses?' Harry asked.

'Father say some boil water.'

'Boil water? Can't true!'

'Yes. Can,' Landis protested.

Harry pretended to flick a pair of horse's reins. 'Tell water go more fast.' He shook the reins again.

Landis put out a hand to stop him. 'No fooling. True. Boil water, same train.'

Harry thought. 'But where fire? Train has fire.' Landis couldn't answer. 'Where hide fire?'

Harry's itch grew, fueled by the Liberty Bell and the mystery of the missing motorcar fire. On Monday and Tuesday he waited at the front gate every spare hour, but no motorcars passed.

On Wednesday he watched the school wagon leaving for the dry-goods store. One of the older fellows from Harry's textile class accompanied Mr. Thomas. Harry considered stealing a ride and hiding under the canvas. But buried in the dark, he wouldn't know his way back if he hopped off, and worse yet, he wouldn't see a thing, and he wanted to see everything. Mr. Thomas tugged at the gate from the street side — it was secure — and drove off.

Harry shuffled to the playing field, kicking leaves as he went. Spectacles waved to him to join his team. Harry wagged his head no. He leaned against a maple near the brick fence and half-watched his friends chase and tumble after the ball.

What he needed was to be able to fly or maybe climb over that wall. A ladder. He needed some sort of ladder.

He had thrown his head back and was gazing through the high cobweb of twigs and leaves when a slow-arcing tree branch bent in the wind for the top of the wall. A playful gust grabbed the limb, rode it downward — well over the bricks — then let the branch loose and whipped it skyward.

Harry's heart quickened. Here was his ladder. The tree!

He looked around. The boys were busy playing. No one would see him. He examined the tree for footholds and handholds. The maple was taller and straighter than the apple trees he was accustomed to, with their low-hanging branches. Reaching the first branch was the hardest. He jumped and missed repeatedly. Finally he was dangling on the bottom-most limb, and wrapping his legs around it, he crawled to the trunk.

The rest was easy. He practiced shinnying up one way and another as he calculated the fastest route to the branch he wanted. He sat for a while watching the street beyond the school fence. To the west the sky was already darkening.

On Thursday, he decided, he'd go motorcar hunting.

Chapter 6

On Thursday

Harry crouched beside his trunk, pawing through its contents: knickers, a sweater his mother had knitted, flannel shirts, and a wool cap. The cap had belonged to his father. Making a fist, he smoothed it from the inside and pulled it over his head.

He had to jump in front of Mrs. Slack's mirror in the laundry room to see himself. His ears stuck out like handlebars and the brim cut off his view of anything above. He couldn't decide — should he wear the cap or not? Then Ralph wandered past on his way to the basins.

'Hey. Nice,' Ralph pointed. Harry smiled. 'Never see before,' Ralph said. 'Why wear today? Your birthday?'

'No,' Harry answered casually. 'Want wear, that's-all.' He pushed the brim farther back over his ears and sauntered out of the laundry.

At lunchtime, as the boys' line angled right for the dining room, Harry bolted left down the corridor past the storeroom, past the employees' cloakroom, and out the door. He ran across the open field as fast as his legs could go.

Soon he reached the maple near the brick fence and leaped. He caught the branch on the first try. He scrambled and twisted his legs around the rough bark, forcing himself up until he hung at last from the bough he'd seen sweep the wall.

Legs swinging, he pulled himself arm over arm away from the tree trunk. But the branch lowered too quickly with his weight. He was going to land inside the wall, not outside.

He swung himself back closer to the trunk. The branch lifted. This time he inched out more slowly. The toes of his shoes were scraping the brick. A little farther and he was suspended by one arm from the tree with the other over the wall. He released the branch and grabbed for the bricks with the second arm.

With more swinging, he scaled the top. He took a satisfied breath and felt for his cap. It was still there.

He threw his leg over, faced the outside, and dropped
— like a ripe fruit — onto a cushion of leaves.

A woman pushing a wicker pram grinned as if she
often saw boys dropping over walls. Harry tipped his
hat. She rolled away and he was tempted to follow,
but then he remembered the road to the church. Perhaps there were more motorcars where he saw the
first. He set out along the wall around the school
grounds.

For an instant he didn't recognize the street. It
blurred with motion. Buggies, handcarts piled with
towers of boxes, and bicycles, their spokes tossing sunlight like handfuls of crumbs, scattered the birds
everywhere. Brown leaves and dust swirled and collapsed. Rivers of people streamed and branched.

When he stepped into the street around an island
of slower-moving people, he felt nearby carriages
rumbling over the cobblestones as though the bottom
were about to fall away beneath his feet.

Bouncing. Jostling. Swaying. Darting. His eyes, his
feet, his very pores prickled with sensation. He'd never
known its equal — not even back home at the village
fair.

He flowed with the crowd until he stood near where
he had first sighted the motorcar, and he broke off. A
black phaeton occupied the spot and the motorcar was

nowhere to be seen. He waited, enjoying the spectacle of color, light, and movement on the street.

A while later, he noticed a man, his hands wavering, joints stiff. The man stopped periodically and poked a cane at the sidewalk before and beside him. He came closer and Harry was amazed to find he was not nearly so old as he imagined. Harry met his gaze, as if to apologize for staring. The man's eyes were opaque. Harry stepped aside. He turned and watched half in pity, half in wonder.

After the blind man, he began feeling impatient. He strained up and down the street. He scoured the house from which the motorcar driver first emerged. By now the phaeton had disappeared and left no sign the motorcar would take its place. He decided to go on and come back later.

He proceeded without hesitation to Mr. Bertie's church. The plain white church was easy to find, silhouetted as it was against a stone-turreted building that rose like a giant marker above it.

Inside, the church looked so much bigger than on Sundays. The pews were emptied of people, the songbooks were straightened and stood upright in their racks, and the black-robed minister was gone.

To the left of the minister's lectern was the huge oak-paneled organ. Harry approached cautiously.

His fingertips skimmed over the polished surface as

though skating on ice. Slowly at first he pulled knobs and pushed the yellowed keys, then wildly, a handful at a time. Magnificent layers of vibrations pulsed from the bench and swelled through his body. He bent from side to side in time to the waves. He was the organist. His arms and torso pumped and swayed to a language he could not speak but read instinctively. He opened his mouth, letting his tongue dance. La la la la la. It was Sunday morning and he was singing with the choir. La la la.

Then someone grabbed a handful of his hair and lifted him off the seat. The wonderful vibrations halted abruptly.

At the end of a long arm a face bulged and writhed. Everything about the face — the cheeks, the forehead, the eyes — spoke anger. Anger. Anger.

Harry was terrified. His arms thrashed and somehow he managed to wriggle his way out of the man's grip. He fled up the aisle, through the double doors, and into the street.

Dodging and squeezing in and out of crowds, he ran without seeing, racing along fences and past buildings. He stopped at a corner to catch his breath. Behind him was an enormous store, across the street a bank, and more stores. Angry Face was nowhere in sight.

He looked again at a store and suddenly he was

clutched with a new fear. Every window, every sign, all of it was new to him. He tried to recognize something, but not a stone looked familiar.

He slumped against the large display window behind him. He was lost. He'd never been lost before.

Resting against the storefront near him was a long-legged, long-armed man. He looked like a spider. Harry watched and waited, pretending to study a small box in the window. Two pink girls in short crisp skirts danced on the lid. The man filled a pipe and lazily drew on the stem. When he'd stiffened his courage, Harry sidled closer.

He pointed to himself. 'Me.' To his ear. 'Ear.' And shook his head. 'No.' He repeated it. 'Me. Ear. No.'

The man screwed his face into a frown, and pulling his gangling arms and legs together, lumbered across the street.

Harry waved. He couldn't let him go. But the man vanished behind a cart into a crowd of people.

Harry's nose watered. He sniffed. His gestures had frightened him off. He'd seen sometimes how the hearing people in Muncy who weren't accustomed to his hands were fearful at first. Next time he wouldn't speak. Not right away.

Several people filed from the store. Harry rejected the first two — too stern. The third, a young woman with velvet bows like bluebirds festooning her hat, smiled prettily at Harry. Harry followed alongside. She glanced down and smiled again. He doffed his cap as she turned into the next doorway.

While Harry stared into the milliner's shop, the pretty lady tried on hats and admired herself in the mirror. Harry waved to her once or twice to remind her he was still there, and she fluttered her hand in return, but she made no move to leave.

There were hats and more hats. Harry yawned and was looking around when he spotted a man with a long plaid neck scarf on the opposite sidewalk. The motorcar man!

He dashed into the road. A horse and wagon swung wide, barely missing him. The driver reared and shook his fist, but Harry didn't have time to consider his narrow escape. He ran joyously for the scarf.

As soon as they were face to face, Harry knew he had the wrong person. He backed away, hot tears stinging the corners of his eyes, while the confused stranger continued up the street.

Harry threw his head back and closed his eyes tight for a long moment. He thought of places he knew, safe places. Slowly he opened them. He blinked.

In the blur above he thought he recognized something. A turret reached for the low-hanging sun. He blinked several times more. Yes. Oh, yes. He could make out the top of the stone tower. Near the church. What good luck!

Eyes up, he hurried as straight for the tower as the city blocks permitted. The closer he came, the harder it was to keep his landmark always in view. Twice he had to retrace his steps and try an alternate route.

At the first sight of the church, he jumped a little jig. For a moment he thought of returning to the store to investigate, but daylight was fading and he knew in a short while he would not have any tower to guide him back.

At least he'd have a peek at the stone building. Sundays with Mr. Bertie, the children entered and exited the church as steadfast as soldiers with no wavering from their fixed course. This was his one chance.

The lower halves of the windows were shuttered from inside. He couldn't see a thing. He poked about and found a door. It opened easily onto a large, dimly lighted room from which several passageways jutted. In the middle squatted a desk similar to Mr. Bertie's. Harry followed one passage to a staircase. On the second floor there were more hallways. He turned down a hallway and into a small room.

Books covered the walls. They were piled on a long table, on a large padded chair, in the corner of a window seat, on a ladder propped against the shelving, and on the floor. He had never seen so many.

He read the spines: *Bits of History, Reynard the Fox, A Tale of Two Cities*, and on and on. His fingers were longing to pull down a book and browse when, in the corner behind the door, he spotted a long pole-like contraption with pincers at the top end. He didn't need to be told this was Landis's claw.

The wood stick was more than twice his height. It wobbled so unsteadily at the bottom he had to stand on the table, brace one foot against a bit of shelf over-hang, and grasp the pole from the middle. By tugging at the cable running the length of the pole he could hold the stick and operate the pincers at the same time.

He aimed the pincers at a book. The book fell on the floor. A second one dropped. But on the next try the pincers clung to a corner. He was busily calculating how to release it into his hand when a balding, thick-nosed gentleman strode into the room.

Harry froze.

The man took the pole from Harry. He picked up the books and skillfully replaced them on the shelf. His lips, tongue, and teeth beat out an erratic rhythm. He nodded to the floor. Harry jumped down.

Despite the man's displeasure, his eyes and hands were open and steady. Harry gestured, 'Me. Ear. No.' He tried to force sound through his lips the way Mr.

Bertie showed him. His neck bulged with the effort.

A quizzical look overtook the man's face. He pulled out a handkerchief and wiped his brow. He pointed for Harry to stay.

The man disappeared and reappeared with paper and pen. "Do you read?" he scribbled.

Harry nodded. He took the pen and wrote "deaf."

The man took the writing pen. "The library is closing." He indicated the long stick. "Come again and I will show you how to use it. It is too noisy when the books fall. You scared me. Also, it is not good for the books."

Harry stared, watching for what he would do next.

He wrote, "Do you go to the deaf school?" Harry was afraid to say yes. What would this man tell Mr. Bertie? "I live not too far from the school," the man continued. "May I walk with you?" He waved once more to the pole. "Our secret," he wrote.

Relieved, Harry signed, 'Thank-you.' He printed on the paper, "All your books?"

The man laughed. He shook his head no. "I am called a librarian. I take care of the books. The city owns the books. Do you like to read?" Harry nodded yes. "Good," he wrote.

Book Man locked up the library. As they strolled together, they shared smiles and gestures, sometimes curious, sometimes comforting, until they came to the school gate. The twilight trees were still. None offered a boy a ride over the brick wall. Harry yanked the bell-pull, while Book Man waited at his side.

Mr. Bertie, Mr. Thomas, and the matrons, followed by several children, hurried to the gate and crowded around. Book Man talked at length to Mr. Bertie. He smiled, shook Harry's hand, shook Mr. Bertie's, then departed with a wave. He faded down the darkening street.

'Much worry,' Mr. Thomas said. He stood tall and grim. 'Already notify police. No wander!'

'I-f you want more books for reading, come see me. I have many,' Mr. Bertie said more kindly.

'Hungry,' Harry responded. He remembered he'd missed lunch and it was the only thing he could think to say.

Mr. Bertie never pressed for any further explanation, though he did restrict Harry to his dormitory room during play periods for two weeks. Harry's punishment passed lightly. Landis, Spectacles, and Cowlick often kept him company. He entertained them with stories of the wonderful organ, Angry Face, the dancing box, the hat store, Book Man, and the blind man.

'Better deaf than blind,' Cowlick commented. 'Yes. Yes,' the others said.

But most of all Harry repeated the story of the tall

claw, showing how it was used and pretending once in a while, to keep his audience amused, to drop a book or two.

'Tell how get outside,' Ralph begged again.

Harry shook his head firmly. 'No.' Out the window the wind gamboled in the tree branches. His secret was a buried treasure. Next time he planned not just to see a motorcar but to ride in one — to the Liberty Bell. He knew he would.

Chapter 7

Whoa

Mr. Bertie seated himself beside Harry. A mirror sat on the desk in front of them. He held up a drawing of an oversized mouth and with a rubber-tipped pointer underlined the position of the tongue and teeth. He pulled a second drawing from behind the first. 'See difference?' He copied the pictures with his own mouth in the mirror and waved his stick between the two.

Yes, Harry nodded his head. He didn't really see, but he was tired of repeating the same words over and over. There were tens of these cards propped on the wainscoting all along the walls of the headmaster's office. He swore the disembodied mouths with their bloated tongues and teeth were jeering at him. He had looked forward to learning to speak, thinking it would be fun. But in fact it was hard, dull work.

'This same s in s-a-l-t. This same s in g-i-r-l-s.'

Harry wondered how Mr. Bertie could look so excited. 'I feel nothing,' he said, 'in teeth, tongue. Nothing. No good. Never learn.'

'With practice become better.' Mr. Bertie's hands moved as though polishing a boot, giving it a couple of extra rubs to emphasize his point. Practice.

'Not care for talking. Happy signing. Me deaf, not hearing.'

'All around hearing. Many, many hearing. Few deaf. You learn for talking with hearing.'

Harry imagined the mouths on the walls as multitudes of hearing, waiting impatiently for him to speak. He and Book Man managed very well using paper and pen, he thought stubbornly.

Mr. Bertie placed Harry's hand over his Adam's apple. 'Follow-me,' he directed.

They plodded through the pronunciation list another time: Seed. As. Case. Song. Bees. Nose. Seeds. No matter what the word, Harry's fingertips detected no difference.

Mr. Bertie stabbed at a word. 'Again.'

Harry's stomach tightened. Girls.

'Again.'

He strained. It was like pushing an invisible mountain from inside. Girls.

'Again.'

His head hurt. Girls. Girls. Girls. Once Mr. Bertie's face lighted with approval, but Harry was more bewildered than ever. He had no idea what he had done, and the light waned. They moved to another word. Cheese. Cheese. Cheese.

Finally Mr. Bertie put aside the cards and lit the candle he kept on the corner of his desk. Harry fixed his eyes on the candle. He puckered and puffed. The flame burned on. He blew again. It flickered and burned.

Mr. Bertie drew the candlestick nearer. Before Harry had been careful. This time he blew in short angry bursts. The taper danced, daring him to try again.

'Why can't?' Harry pleaded.

'Blowing always hard.' Mr. Bertie looked down. His gaze was gentle. 'Must many times. Hurry not good. Mix-up. Take time. You will learn.'

Harry sank back in his chair. Mechanically, he went through the motions — pucker and blow, pucker and blow — all the while keeping his eye on Mr. Bertie's vest pocket. Mr. Bertie, meantime, concentrated all his attention on Harry, as if he could will his pupil to learn if he were determined enough.

At last. The watch was pulled from the vest pocket. Harry would have bounded out the door, except that Mr. Bertie put a hand to his shoulder and held him back.

'No hurry,' he said. His eyes opened wide. 'I have surprise for you.'

A surprise? What sort of surprise could there be for him? He'd done so poorly on his speech lessons.

The headmaster put on his wrap and told Harry to find his. They went outside, around the school building, and to the stable.

Mr. Bertie led a gentle old nag from her stall and into the paddock. Harry recognized her. The other children called her 'Star' for the white blaze on her forehead. The school horses were used to haul wagons and carriages, but Star usually stood idle beneath a tree or rummaged for grass.

The schoolmaster slapped Star on the buttocks and she loped round and round the enclosure like a trick horse Harry saw once in Muncy. Then Mr. Bertie placed Harry's fingertips against his voice box.

Harry balked. Another lesson, he thought. He scowled as he faced his teacher.

Mr. Bertie's face twinkled a knowing smile. 'Not watch me. Watch horse.' He turned Harry's shoulders toward Star.

Very soon Harry felt a deep rumble in Mr. Bertie's

throat and moments later Star stopped. Harry looked to Mr. Bertie for an explanation. Bertie winked. 'Watch.' He started Star up, repeated the exercise, and once more the horse came to a leisurely standstill.

People talked to people. But Mr. Bertie was talking to a horse! Harry's irritation was turning to excitement. 'More,' he urged, and Mr. Bertie obliged willingly.

The questions poured out. 'How make horse stop? Show-me how? Can I?' Harry begged.

Mr. Bertie's hands signed a wide ribbon pulled from his mouth. 'I yelled,' he explained.

'But how?' Harry's signs were impatient.

'Watch more.' Mr. Bertie pulled Harry's hands, one to his stomach and the other a few inches from his mouth. As Mr. Bertie yelled, his stomach rose, tensed sharply, and at the same time a small wind brushed across Harry's palm.

'Feel something!' Harry said.

'Wind,' said Bertie. 'Talking really wind. I suck-in. Like-this.' His stomach ballooned. 'Mouth.' His mouth formed a half-open circle. 'And push with stomach.' The breeze swept Harry's hand. 'You try.'

Harry positioned his hands on himself. But when his stomach swelled, the air seemed to be stuck. Bertie moved the hand higher on his stomach. Still nothing happened.

'Me again.' The headmaster took back Harry's hands. 'Try throat now.' Then he yelled. Once. Twice. Three times. Harry shifted his hands between Bertie's stomach, throat, and mouth again and again. 'Need three hands,' Mr. Bertie teased.

He was feeling for the vibrations, trying to track them like a hunting dog in pursuit of quarry. He held out his palm. 'More. More,' he demanded. The headmaster yelled several times.

He could see it now. The air was a pliable substance, pushed and pinched, stretched and shaped, in the throat and mouth. If only there weren't so many steps to remember.

He removed his hands from Mr. Bertie. There was nothing left but for him to try it. One hand on the bump, the other on his middle. Push. He looked to Mr. Bertie. No? He tried again. Again he watched the headmaster. He was becoming frantic. It was just too much to remember. He repeated the process a third time. Air in, out a little, more . . . push!

He felt the rightness of it even before the smile widened the old man's face. 'I know! I know!' he tapped his forehead. 'Hurry. Hurry before forget.'

Mr. Bertie ran as fast as his weight would permit to the horse and smacked her rump. In. Out. Push. Harry's fingers tingled. His entire throat was quivering. Then he hoped.

Star stopped and nuzzled a nearby fence post. Harry hesitated, disbelieving. Then he jumped and jumped, clapping his hands. Mr. Bertie reached out. 'Congratulations,' he said.

'Want more,' Harry said.

They practiced all afternoon, losing track of the hours.

'Word-name for yell W-h-o-a. W-h-o-a first talking word,' Mr. Bertie told him. Harry fingerspelled the word to himself. So that's what he was saying.

He yelled, "Whoa! Whoa!"

Mr. Bertie covered his ears. 'Much loud. Much loud,' he laughed.

When Mr. Thomas called them to dinner, Harry pleaded to continue. 'Poor horse. Tired,' Mr. Bertie answered. He took Star's harness and headed her in the direction of the stable.

During his next speech lesson a day or two later, Harry pretended to be extra bored with blowing the candle. Then, as if the idea suddenly struck him, the headmaster said, 'Come-on. See horse,' and donned his coat.

Harry didn't need a second invitation. He yelled and yelled, and when he was refreshed, he and Mr. Bertie walked back to the school building to face the candle together.

Chapter 8

Thanksgiving Football

Harry poked his head out the window again. Mr. Thomas and the senior boys were setting up the goalposts. They lined up on either side and leaned into the wood frame, pushing it up hand over hand until it wobbled uncertainly in the ground. Several fellows shoveled the dirt piles back into the holes and tamped them down.

Harry crossed the fingers of both hands and shook them to ward off a dark cloud that hovered over the playing field. 'Go-away. Tomorrow fine. Not today.'

Landis also was kneeling in the open window. He laughed. 'Think those deaf? No, no. They not understand signs.'

'Bah! You think know all. Your mind has weak knees,' Harry taunted. He staggered around the dormitory room weaving between the beds.

Landis had him cornered when Mrs. Slack emerged from the laundry. She half-signed, half-mouthed the words. 'No fight. I-f bad boys, no turkey.' Harry ignored her and took advantage of the interruption to escape from the corner.

Besides, he didn't care about turkey. He danced from foot to foot, waiting for Landis to lunge. What he cared about was the football game — not their usual free-for-all but a real game, with goalposts and a grid — between Mr. Bertie's seniors and Harding Academy.

A rude tug yanked him to his senses. 'Close window. I-f catch cold, more work for me,' Mrs. Slack ordered. She drew herself up and folded her arms. Harry scurried to the window.

The two boys washed, dressed, and went running for the football field. Landis complained about missing breakfast. 'Good for you,' Harry said. 'Stomach more big — more for turkey.'

Several other boys already were at the picket fencing. Even the fence had been erected for the occasion. They watched Mr. Thomas chalk off the field in large white rectangles, running one into the other.

Mr. Bertie, looking simply grand with his gray shock

of hair stuffed under a purple-and-gold-striped knit cap and laced into a sporting vest and trousers, cantered from fence to goalpost issuing instructions. His middle jiggled so, a pound or two looked as if it could unhitch and roll off on its own.

The headmaster called all the boys at the fence over. He handed them each a big sack to tie about their waists and told them to pick up the debris scattered on the playing field.

The boys quickly turned their chore into a game. They dived for leaves. They vied for twigs and stones. Someone stepped on a bag, maybe even his own, and they tripped and sank in a body. Soon their loads grew so heavy the sacks dragged, and still they romped like tethered goats around their anchors. But when the clusters of strangers began trailing onto the field their giddiness evaporated. The boys finished up and lugged their sacks to the trash heap on the other side of the stable.

Hurrying back, Harry saw bicycles, horses, and carriages filling the spacious drive, though no motorcars. Men in bowler hats and handlebar mustaches were walking to the field accompanied by children in curls and white ruffles and women in puff-sleeved suits. They arranged and rearranged themselves along the fencing. A few carried cameras. Farther along the fence an elderly man half-reclined in a rolling chair.

Harry felt a keen sense of loss. The playing field had become as familiar as the hills and pond of the farm for him. Surrounded by intruders, he didn't know it any more.

The Bertie team, followed by the lower-form boys, gathered at an end of the field away from the crowd. They watched the Harding players, who watched them. Ralph wiggled his overlarge ears in return, and Harry giggled so hard the tears came.

'Hey,' waved LeRoy Cole, captain of the team and not one to waste an audience, 'know how deaf can win?'

One of the other players ventured an answer. 'Rapid Heart say hearing very good play. Say we must work hard.'

'No, no. Hearing easy lose. Know how?' LeRoy smirked. 'During play we yell. Mix-up their minds. Not mix-up deaf minds. Prove deaf better.'

Everyone laughed and jostled. LeRoy opened his mouth wide and the younger boys pumped out whatever sounds they could make, which attracted more stares.

While the boys horsed around, Mr. Bertie and another man wearing a similar vest stood aside talking. Finally the second man picked up a flared horn and pointed it at the crowd.

Mr. Bertie waved his team closer. The boys watched

anxiously to see what rules they would play by today. Eleven players on a side; no substitutions except for injured players; no kicking, no tripping, no fighting; five points for a field goal, four for a touchdown, and two for a goal after the touchdown. 'Understand?' Bertie asked. They nodded their approval.

The Harding team filed two abreast behind their captain onto the playing field. Each boy wore a red armband and a few wore head protectors. The Bertie boys, in contrast, straggled out. The man with the megaphone hurried to the Bertie team and after some confusion a twelfth player was sent to the fence. The Harding boys were smiling to the crowd. We look foolish, Harry thought angrily. He wished the game would hurry up.

Harding won the toss. Harry tensed himself for the frantic charge after the ball. But the Harding team linked arms and locked themselves in a human barricade around the carrier. It was slick as butter. They cut a furrow down the middle of the Bertie players, turning them aside. The people at the sidelines were screaming so loud Harry could feel the waves of sound beating on him like a heavy rain. Harding made the touchdown for four points and a goal after the touchdown.

Now it was Bertie's turn. The football moved. There was a headfirst rush and LeRoy broke loose. Landis,

Spectacles, and Harry clung to each other, leaping with excitement. Then LeRoy plummeted. He struggled free on the next play and the next. Once he dragged his attackers several feet. But in the end he was too big and too heavy to outrun them. When the other side took possession of the ball, LeRoy fought mightily to reach the carrier. He couldn't touch him. The crowd surged along the fence, chasing the red scarves, as Harding steadily gained yardage. They scored again.

The boys turned to each other in dismay. 'What you think A-c-a-d-e-m-y mean?' said Spectacles.

Harry shrugged. All their bragging hadn't prepared him for this. 'New to me,' he said.

'Think hearing word,' Cowlick said.

A cold thin drizzle came down. The neatly laid-out grid changed to muck. In the pile-ups there was more and more slugging and hair-pulling. A Bertie player limped off the field.

The younger boys began drifting away. 'Play with us,' Cowlick urged.

'I want stay,' Harry said.

'Finish. We soon lose,' Cowlick answered.

On the grid the two schools were facing off. LeRoy Cole, ordinarily so slow to anger, picked up a hunk of mud and hurled it at the opposite line. A player caught it in the eye and the teams piled up without ever touching the ball. Mr. Bertie, Mr. Thomas, and a couple of other men had to pry the boys off each other. The megaphone man and Mr. Bertie escorted LeRoy out of the game.

LeRoy grimaced apologetically. 'Can't get through. Rough,' he said, his eyes glued to the Harding team. Both teams retired to the sidelines for a rest period. Several boys Harry's age and with the same red bandanas tied to their arms passed buckets of water over the picket fence. 'Smart,' LeRoy added. It was admiration, not anger.

Harry felt it as well. 'But deaf smart, true,' he said, as much for himself as for LeRoy.

The players were taking their positions in line. Tired of craning around other spectators to see, Harry decided to climb his maple tree for an easier view. Up here the football field was a different world.

William Freeman, who replaced LeRoy, tucked the ball under his arm. He sprinted for the goal — and in a beeline for his tacklers. Harry pounded the tree branch. Go around. It was so clear. They should run anywhere — back and forth, even in circles, to the goal — just not in straight lines.

Harding was carrying the ball now. Harry leaned far out on the limb. From the air their wall was actually a V-shape configuration, like wild ducks flying south. The lead duck had to keep looking back to stay in formation. Many times he flew too far in front of his teammates, leaving an opening. Harry nearly lost his grip. That was it!

He scrambled down the tree and ran to his friends.

'Where you? Looking for you,' Landis demanded.

'We can win! I know how!'

Landis pointed a finger at his ear and drew large circles. 'You crazy.'

'No, no. Watch.' Harry told the boys what he'd seen from the tree and presented his plan.

Cowlick patted Harry on the back. 'Good idea. Like.'

Heads cocked, arms swinging, they walked over to the water boys. Harry pointed to the one he thought might be their leader. 'You. Me.' He pretended to run carrying a football and gestured to the far playing field.

The water boy signaled to another fellow. They talked, hands cupped over their mouths. At last the first boy turned to Harry. He repeated Harry's gestures. You. Me. Running with the ball.

'O-K. We play,' Harry said to the others. He grinned.

The two leaders waved their teams to the unmarked field. They counted off players. Enough for eight on a side. The Red captain flipped a coin. The water boys won.

The ball went into play and Harry held his breath. Just as he hoped, the Red players dropped back and re-formed in a V.

He signaled Cowlick and Landis to move to his rear. They charged. At the moment of impact Cowlick and Landis grabbed his trousers from behind. They lifted and shoved him up and over the lead Red player. There was not a moment to spare. Landis and Cowlick already were going down, but Harry was flying. Head lowered, legs thrashing, he dived into the ball carrier and collided with his stomach. The Red captain dropped.

They tried their maneuver a second time. A third. Up and over. Up and over. It was working! Harry punched Landis's shoulder and clasped his hands in a show of victory.

It was their turn with the ball. 'Make T-D same-way-as Red,' Spectacles argued in the huddle.

'No. No good V,' Harry said. 'What i-f they pull-up same we d-o to them? We lose same-way. Must have new idea.' He gestured the boys closer. 'Wrong carry ball straight. Must go-around. Red can't find.'

They moved to the line. Cowlick rolled the ball back to Harry. Harry grabbed and ripped away from both teams like a gust of wind. He zigzagged past one player. He circled another and jumped out of the path of still another. It was as if he were at home, leaping, skidding, on rubber joints in and out of cow tracks, until someone brought him to the ground with a flying tackle. Dazed, Harry rose to his knees and surveyed the field. Less than half to go.

On the next run the Reds converged on Harry, and he collapsed easily.

On the third try he was determined to stay up. He looped far to the left. Two of the Reds, followed by their teammates, had spotted him, and they were running to cut him off. He picked up speed but the gap was closing. A Red leaped for him and he side-stepped, still running. The boy landed and slid face first in the mud. Suddenly players from both teams threw themselves on top of the downed player.

Harry checked. He still had the ball. He was still up. He ran faster, feet and heart pounding. Another ten yards to go. Five. He didn't dare look to see who was chasing him. The remaining few inches slipped beneath his feet.

Harry raised the ball aloft. 'I d-i-d! I d-i-d!'

After that the Reds made no more mistakes, and the game was soon stalemated. Neither side was able to score. Then Harry's pants tore out of Cowlick's grasp. They were trampled as the water boys rushed over for a touchdown to tie the score.

The senior game was breaking up. People walked by on their way to the carriages. A few stopped to watch. LeRoy stood on the side, shamefaced. 'H-a-r-d-i-n-g school win. Twenty. We zero,' he said.

'Try V,' Spectacles urged again.

'No good copy hearing,' Harry countered. 'Must think what deaf can d-o very good.' He pulled at Cowlick. 'Something for you. Follow carefully what I say.'

When they left the huddle, Harry hailed LeRoy. 'No sad. Soon happy. You see.'

The two teams stood toe to toe. Landis started the ball in motion. Harry stretched to receive it. He enclosed his right hand inside his left elbow and pumped his legs with all his might. He dropped back, then swung left in a zigzagging arc. Landis and Ralph followed at his heels. The Reds swarmed after them. One of the bigger boys caught up and reached. Harry ducked and kept on running. Landis tumbled.

Now Ralph fell behind. Harry fought the urge to give in. Cowlick needed more time. He wheeled and drew the Reds deeper into his own territory.

At last someone spun him around and threw him to the ground. His body curled around his clenched fist. He could see the Red captain's shock when the other boys crashed down on him.

The Red captain jerked furiously at his teammates. He pointed the way to Cowlick, who was carrying the real ball. They lunged in Cowlick's direction, but too late. Cowlick made the touchdown and threw his arms in the air. Victory!

The senior boys rushed onto the field, embracing and clapping. LeRoy helped Harry to his feet. He was smiling from ear to ear.

Harry gave LeRoy a playful cuff. 'Happy now?'

'You win. But I lose,' LeRoy said.

'No,' Harry answered. 'One. One. Deaf win one. Hearing win one.'

The Red captain approached Harry and extended a grimy hand. Harry shook it. He took a deep breath. In his heart he knew he had come out more than even.

The rest of the hearing crowd thinned quickly. Their carriages and bicycles rolled through the brick gates, leaving little evidence of their visit. Only the giant goalposts remained against the gray sky.

Harry and Landis loped toward the school building. Landis broke into Harry's thoughts. 'Why give Cowlick ball? Why not give-me?'

Harry grinned and pinched Landis's fat middle. 'You right. You big. Hide ball better. Next your time.'

Landis went running ahead. 'Come!' he waved to Harry. 'Afraid turkey bird soon fly-away.'

Chapter 9

'M-e-r-r-y Christmas!'

The dapple-gray horse snorted two white clouds. He strained and the buggy started rolling. Landis hung out the open cab and threw his arms madly. 'Bye. Happy h-o-l-i-d-a-y! See you next three weeks.'

'Good time! Good time!' Harry signed after him.

The carriage hesitated at the school gate and disappeared around the corner. Lucky Landis, Harry thought. His friend was already nearly home, while he had a two-hour train ride ahead of him.

He unwrapped his arm from the large outdoor lamp and hopped off the stone banister. Inside the building the corridors were empty. The instructors and housekeeping staff had said their farewells at breakfast. The slates were wiped clean. And all morning the springboard was filled with luggage and children, making several round trips to the railroad station.

He met Miss Bertie coming down the east corridor. She stopped. 'Have good rest. Finish rest, come-back ready work hard. Yes?' Harry nodded his head agreeably. Miss Bertie ruffled his hair and chucked his chin. He could feel his neck prickle. 'Good boy for mother, father. Yes? Bye-bye.' She wafted down the hall.

Harry forgot for a moment he was on his way to see her father.

The door to Mr. Bertie's office stood ajar. He knocked, poking his face inside. Mr. Bertie looked up from his papers. 'Excuse, talk?' Harry asked.

'Come-in,' the headmaster motioned. 'Think you go home.'

'Soon my time. Before leave, want know anyone ask for pin?' Harry had found the pin by the fence the day after the football game. On the brooch's face a shepherd piped gaily to a maiden. Two curly lambs rested at their feet. As soon as his eyes lighted on the pin, he knew his mother should have it. If only no one claimed it.

'No. No one ask.' Mr. Bertie reached in his desk drawer and pulled out a woman's brooch. 'Pretty. Funny no one looking for.'

Harry stepped closer. 'Maybe who lost it think someone find pin and carry home. Think lost always. Give-up,' he added hopefully.

'Yes. Maybe right.' Mr. Bertie paused. 'I think hold long enough. I-f like pin, you may have.'

'Take home?'

'You find. You keep.' Mr. Bertie handed him the brooch.

'I give my mother. Thank-you. Thank-you very, very!' Harry felt as if his dessert platter had been heaped with an extra mound of ice cream. He raced out of the office and upstairs to pack the pin.

As he went to put it away he noticed the clasp was bent. He straightened it. The word "France" was inscribed underneath. His mother would be so pleased when she saw that "France" written on the back.

He wrapped the pin with the same brown paper and string that he saved from his drawing pencils and slipped it into the bottom of his carpetbag next to the other presents for his family. For Ray he had his picture of the school that Mr. Bertie had returned to him, little string purses made from waste scraps he and Agnes found in the textile shop for his sisters, and for his father a likeness of himself. Mrs. Slack had lent him her mirror so he could draw it.

He pushed the bag together and held it closed with a knee while he fastened the leather straps. On went his wool cap and a coat. He hefted his overburdened case. He was ready to go.

Mr. Thomas was just returning from the train station. Agnes stood by the curb with her bags. Harry waved hello but she hardly noticed. He tried again. 'Carry home cloth. Inside.' He pointed to his case. 'Will give sisters surprise.' Agnes made no reply. Her face looked taut and her lips pressed in a straight line, as if she were uncomfortable, or maybe angry.

'Mad?'

'No, no,' Agnes said and climbed in the wagon beside another girl. Harry wondered what was wrong. Usually she was so friendly. He'd learned a lot from her in the afternoons about what the girls did in their part of the school. He boarded from the rear with two senior boys.

'Sick?' he asked.

'No, no.'

'What?'

Now he was certain she was annoyed. 'Not like train ride, that's-all. Many people, crowded,' she said.

Harry waited for more, hoping to understand, but Agnes's clasped hands lay still in her lap. They would say no more. He turned to the two or three children remaining on the steps. 'Good-bye.' 'See soon.' 'M-e-r-r-y Christmas!' they flailed.

When they reached the station, Mr. Thomas ushered them onto the waiting train and vanished. The older boys took seats together at the front of the car. Harry took a seat alone, and the two girls sat catercorner behind him.

Like a doll on a string, Harry's head pivoted, drinking in his surroundings. The first coach he'd traveled in to Philadelphia he remembered as a narrow, overtall compartment with uncomfortable slat seats. But this train was luxury itself. Wood curlicues and scallops carved into the armrests, on the luggage racks, over the windows, on the doors between coaches, and along the ceiling gleamed with fresh polish. A long runner carpeted the floor in the same flowered design as the upholstered chairs. The arched windows matched the curved tops of the seats, and each window boasted an individual movable shade. Cheery sunlight poured in the second tier of windows above the luggage racks.

He pulled the shade up and down several times until he found the right position; then, wriggling with pleasure, he settled back in his overstuffed chair. A rich man couldn't have it any better than this, he imagined. He folded his hands behind his head. Even the ceiling tiles were decorated.

A lady carrying a wicker basket loaded with packages rested briefly next to Harry's seat. A long plume draped from her hat. She walked like a bird, mincing a few steps, halting, pecking at the air around her, her plume bobbing. Harry heaved a sigh of relief when she laid her cloak on a seat farther up the aisle. She'd be the sort who made children sit up straight.

A hearing boy about his age passed through, wearing a tray on a strap slung around his neck. His sign read PEANUTS — 2¢. Harry dug deep into his pocket for two pennies.

Harry shucked a shell and popped the warm peanuts into his mouth. Delicious. He was still admiring the coach when he saw Agnes signaling to him. She talked in frantic little gestures beside her cheek. 'Look-up. Behind.'

He turned. The conductor was squinting and beckoning impatiently. He searched his pockets again and handed over his ticket. The conductor punched it and moved on.

He reached over and tapped Agnes's knee. 'Not see. Thank-you. Wonderful train! First time much pretty!' The man opposite Agnes leaned into the aisle for a better look at Harry. Harry plunged on, ignoring the man. 'Up-there see chairs go-round, round. Want sit-in, but all full. Maybe later, someone get-off train. You, me can try. O-K?'

Now several people were straining to see. Agnes's face turned crimson. She stared alongside Harry out the window. He looked over his hands at the people bent toward him and stopped. He turned to the window, too. He felt clumsy and awful and angry.

At last the steam engine lurched forward, spewing gray clouds that furled around the train. Through the misty stream he saw a boy and a girl with a dog running along the embankment. He didn't wave back. He just watched. Naked trees replaced buildings. As they slid backward, new ones stepped up to take their place.

When he thought it was safe, he looked away from the countryside. The hearing people were talking or reading. A few shucked peanuts. Up front the two Bertie seniors gazed absent-mindedly at the other passengers. They exchanged glances and very occasionally a gesture, so faint that probably to the hearing they seemed no different from anyone else riding the train.

Harry tried in vain to catch Agnes's attention. He wanted to let her know he hadn't deliberately embarrassed her, but she refused to see him.

He wouldn't do it, but he also wanted to tell her she was silly.

The steady churning of the train beneath him was lulling him to sleep. He closed his eyes and pictured everyone in his family: Baby Anna in her bonnets and outstretched arms always begging to be picked up; Veve in pigtails, dragging a rag doll with her everywhere; Ray, so serious, hurt-looking — how Harry loved to make him laugh; his fun-loving mother, quick to joke or pretend; and his father, like Ray, serious, even timid — he loved beautiful things.

His father would have been annoyed with him, too, like Agnes. He could see him smiling humbly at the hearing, preferring to go among them unnoticed. What would Landis do? he mused wistfully.

He yawned. His mother wasn't afraid of them either. Once she scared away some hearing boys who were making fun of him. Somehow he'd always guessed the hearing were different, but he hadn't known how. Then one day on one of those rare trips into the village, he'd been sitting on a bench outside the general store sucking on ginger candy with Veve and Ray when three boys about Ray's and his age crowded around.

He'd said, 'Hello. My name H-a-r-r-y. What your name?'

The biggest of the three threw his arms around wildly. Harry'd understood immediately the boy was pretending to imitate him. The other two held their bellies and pranced, their mouths hanging open. They moved in closer. The big one made faces. Harry stood up. He knew if he didn't hit one of them soon he'd cry.

Suddenly his mother came between them. She pointed indignantly at the boys. 'Away! Away!' Her face was menacing. The boys turned tail and scooted around a building and watched from a safe distance.

77

His mother had hugged him and wiped his face. 'No ashamed. Never,' she said. 'Sometimes hearing mind act strange. I-f afraid, always ashamed. I-f ignore, happy inside.' His mother certainly was that, he thought, happy inside.

On a later visit, he and Ray settled their differences with the hearing boys in a fist fight behind the general store. His mother made him promise not to tell his father. Another time they made friends. After that, whenever their wagon drove to town, he and his brother wandered to the river, where they were certain to find at least one of the boys. They played together on the worn footbridge and traded candies, or watched stilt-legged insects walk atop the water, or heaved stones and broken tree branches into the slow-moving Muncy River. He and Ray gave the biggest boy the sign-name 'Freckles,' for the little brown flakes sprinkled over his nose and cheeks.

The braking train jostled into his daydreams. When he looked up, the senior boys were gone, along with Agnes's seat companion. Agnes was bundled in her wrap and sat clutching her parcel. The train lurched once more and stopped. Agnes and the bird lady stood up. Agnes stiffened as she approached. Harry bowed his head lightly, not enough to call attention, and she cast a relieved sideways smile.

When Agnes stepped off the train several people

embraced her, a man who might have been her father, an elderly woman in dark clothes, and two other girls, both bigger than Agnes. The man took her bags and brought a wagon over to the platform and helped the old lady up to a seat beside him. The girls climbed in. And Agnes's wagon was gone. No one signed to her, not once.

The placard at the next stop said ALBION. A few short miles and they'd be arriving in Muncy. As he recognized more and more of the rolling farmland, Harry's heart pounded so it was bursting. He slapped his cap against the armrest, keeping time with the pulsing rhythm of the train. Hurry. Hurry. Hurry, he slapped.

The train followed the river valley, passing almost within sight of his family's farm. It swept around a wide curve in the river. When they reached the last bend, Harry scrambled for his belongings and bolted for the coach door. The train crawled the last few feet to the station.

There they were! He could see his family. They were walking alongside looking for him. His father carried Anna asleep on his shoulder. Harry leaned to a window and waved joyously.

Suddenly he remembered his cap. He'd dropped it somewhere. He dashed back and found it beside his seat. He bent to pick it up and glanced again at the other passengers. Then he stomped his foot — boldly, firmly — and waited. Everyone looked.

He signed in his most eloquent gestures, 'I going home for Christmas vacation. M-e-r-r-y Christmas to all!' He waved good-bye.

A man in glasses waved back. A woman. Several others. Soon the entire compartment was waving.

'Good-bye! Good-bye!' He doffed his cap and bounded from the train.

Chapter 10

Home

Harry rushed from the train expecting to be resewn into his family as if the tear in their lives never existed. Yet almost immediately he sensed an unfamiliar distance. Anna stirred on her father's shoulder, and when Harry put out his hands to hold her, she screwed up her face and clung to her father. Even Veve and Ray hung behind their mother.

His mother kissed him, and after she had inspected him she said, 'Don't-know you. Before here. Now here.' She pointed to two different places on her arm, one higher than the other. 'Grow fast!' Harry tried to look proud, but inside he wished he were little enough to crawl into his daddy's arms like Anna.

His mother sent the other children to the rear of the

wagon and made room for him on the front seat for the drive home. Harry leaned back to offer the bag of peanuts and found Veve sitting in his usual place on the end opposite Ray. She rode the erratic wagon shakes and jiggles with the poise of someone who knew that spot well.

Suddenly he noticed the horse pulling the wagon. It was different — not their horse. 'Where P-r-u-d-y?' he said, his irritation swelling.

His mother answered. 'Home. P-r-u-d-y old. Tired. We buy new horse.'

'Preacher help. Talk to hearing for us. Good price,' his father said. 'Without preacher, maybe more.'

'Not write you about?' his mother asked. Harry shook his head no. 'We forget. Sorry.' What else did they forget, he wondered sullenly.

Harry barely took the time to drop his carpetbag. As soon as they arrived home, he hurried up the two flights of stairs to his room. He was afraid to look, afraid that here, too, he would feel a difference. But the door leaned open and in the half-light of the dimming afternoon he could make out his low trundle bed heaped high with the same feather comforter, the funny wide rocker that was like a bench where he used to put the barn kittens and rock until they jumped off, and books, lots of books, strewn among the same broken chairs, and the same aging trunk of musty clothes.

He flopped on his bed, savoring the smells of old wood, dust, and drying corn and string beans. He loved it here atop the farmhouse. He loved to lie on the bare floor between his bed and the window, his head propped on a few books, reading about Revolutionary soldiers and early settlers or watching the birds dart across his box to the sky.

The heat that had built steadily with the climbing sun was starting to leak out the chinks and cracks of the attic into the dark. Harry shuddered as he stripped down to his flannels, but the underside of his comforter was still warm from the daytime heat captured between the covers. He snuggled down and fell asleep.

When he came downstairs the next morning, his father and Ray were nowhere to be seen. His mother and Veve were kneading bread, while the baby patted smaller rounds of dough. Anna looked up and hid behind her mother.

'Where father and Ray?'

'Work on apple trees. Time for cutting. Some p-r-u-n-i-n-g,' his mother answered.

'Want milk cows?'

'Finish. Ray d-i-d.'

'I see.' Harry frowned. Those were his jobs.

83

'I think school let-you sleep late,' his mother said, winking. Harry wished her look were disapproving instead. At least he would have felt he had something useful he was supposed to do. His mother wiped her hands on her apron and pumped a basin of water for him. Anna followed after her skirts, peering around occasionally to see if he'd gone yet.

Harry washed and after he finished eating his warmed-up rolls and ham, he wandered about the farm aimlessly. In the barn he teased the cats with pieces of hay. He poked around in the sawdust at the icehouse. Less than a third of the cakes of ice were left. He remembered chopping them with his father when the pond at the bottom of the hill froze over last winter. He looked out at the few high mounds of clouds riding in a bright sky. This December was so mild and he had to return to school after the first. He wouldn't be cutting ice this year.

He saddled Prudy and took her out for a run, but her energy was quickly spent and he turned back. They loped to the apple orchard. When Harry left for school the trees had been heavy with fruit. Their rosy bloom was gone now. His father and Ray both hailed him warmly, then continued their pruning. Harry tied Prudy and she nosed the rotting apples beneath the tree.

His father wielded the only saw. Ray was daubing

the fresh-cut stumps with a stick wrapped in cloth, so Harry stirred the little pot of thick tar. But he was soon bored and he drifted away. He swung on a few branches and watched a chipmunk struggle to carry a fallen apple. As he studied Ray, working side by side with their father, a wave of homesickness swept over him like the ones he'd experienced when he first went to Mr. Bertie's.

He gestured good-bye and, leading Prudy, trudged the steep slope to the barn. After he unsaddled her and let her go in the paddock, he stayed to watch the roan.

The new horse strained to wrap its loose-fitting lips around a clump of grass just out of reach. Harry approached slowly. He ripped up a handful of weeds, which the horse gobbled.

'You beautiful,' Harry signed. He patted the horse's head. The eyes were big and forlorn.

The roan leaned over the top rail and nudged Harry with his powerful head. Taken by surprise, Harry laughed. He yanked another stalk of grass and the horse ate greedily. After each fist was emptied, he waited until the horse nearly knocked him over to produce the next batch. He was enjoying the game when suddenly the roan was sated. It kicked up its heels and galloped in the opposite direction, tail flying.

'No go. Stay,' Harry waved sorrowfully.

The horse circled the fence and was sweeping past.

Impulsively, Harry sucked in a bellyful of air. He
pushed out the air slowly at first, then harder, ending
with a stiff upward push.

The roan pricked up his ears and obediently
stopped.

It was like a miracle! Somehow Harry had always
imagined he needed Mr. Bertie there with him for his
trick to work. He slid between the horizontal bars and
ran to the horse with a big handful of weeds, and the
roan courteously lapped at them.

He had the horse repeat the exercise several times,
and then a few more times to be sure. Their perform-
ance was flawless. Harry was elated. He brushed and
combed the roan with extra care, and Prudy, too, so
she wouldn't feel left out. He said the word over and
over to himself with each stroke. "Whoa." "Whoa."
He patted Prudy. 'New friend,' he signed to her,
'name W-h-o-a. Good name, you think?' Prudy shook
her mane and nuzzled his pocket for the carrot hid-
den there.

That afternoon Harry didn't wait to be invited. He
threw himself into Ray's tasks as if they were his own.
They mulched row upon row of apple trees, together
they sawed and chopped enough firewood to last
probably into the next week, and by the time they
milked the cows again, the stiffness between them
softened, and they teased and joked like old times.

'Learn wonderful new game! F-o-o-t-b-a-l-l,' Harry said as they rested on a grassy knoll.

Ray repeated the word. 'F-o-o-t-b-a-l-l. Never see before. What?'

'Wait. Show-you.' Harry sprang to his feet and hurried to the house, where he cajoled a rag from his mother to wrap around a bunch of leaves as a football. He tried to describe a scrimmage line and show Ray how to take the ball from him from behind, but the leaves kept falling out and Ray looked more perplexed than he was at the outset. Harry gave up and threw the leaking rag at Ray.

Ray collected an armful of leaves and heaped them on his brother, stuffing them into his shirt collar and down his back. 'This not new. I know how play!'

They scuffled good-naturedly, then sprawled in the leaves.

'You see Freckles? Other boys?' Harry asked.

'No. Father mad.' Ray's eyes and lips bulged; his fingers wriggled before his face as though scintillating with sparks of fire. Harry nodded appreciatively. He knew his father. 'Last time see no boys anywhere,' Ray said. 'Maybe in school,' he added.

'Yes. Hard find during winter. Think in school all day, like me now.'

'How school feel? You like?' Ray asked.

'School same —' Harry searched for the right

words. He wanted to say it was like the deaf picnic they attended once a year, because they had fun, but on the other hand, they did have to work. 'Little-bit same f-a-i-r. Many interesting things. New. New. Always something d-o. Never bored. But little-bit same preacher visit. Must listen.

'Teachers all hearing. But can sign. Same Preacher Ervin. Funny hearing. Scare easy. Once during study hour all boys, girls watch clock. Perfect 7:45 — all drop book on floor. Teacher jump! Face white, then red!' Harry laughed heartily. 'I will always remember.'

'I think not like school. Father says read all time.'

Harry jumped to his feet. 'No. No. You like. I know! Not all time books. One in morning. Sometimes read, sometimes write. Or numbers. But most time learn work. Carpenter, printer, tailor.' Ray still seemed unconvinced. Harry drew Ray closer to him. 'I want you come to deaf school with me. First time see many, many deaf. Wonderful. Make strong friends.' Ray smiled, but Harry could see it was without understanding. He hugged his brother. 'You will come. You see.'

Ray shrugged, bewildered. 'Don't-know.'

Just then a tiny shower of leaves trickled down on them. It was Anna. Her bonnet strings were untied and she was sucking a fat thumb. 'Horse,' she said. Horse was her favorite game before Harry went away.

Instantly, Harry dropped to his knees and burrowed under Ray. Ray rode his shoulders and they galloped circles around Anna, stopping often to rear and throw the rider. Anna watched, delighted. Harry stopped once to rest and Anna pouted. 'Horse.' Harry obliged over and over — 'Horse,' she asserted — until he was exhausted.

Their chores finished early, in the evening they sat in the kitchen by the wood stove. Harry thought how wonderful it was to be in a kitchen again. At Mr. Bertie's the children weren't allowed. Here the kitchen was the center of the house. All the other downstairs rooms and the hallway to the upstairs opened onto it. It was the point from which everyone departed and the place where everyone returned.

His father sat in his rocker bent toward the oil lamp, reading a book of Grimms' tales. Anna waited in his lap and Veve sat on the floor beside him.

Veve tapped his knee for at least the third or fourth time. 'Finished?'

Harry's father brought his thumb to his lips and drew a short line, 'Patience,' and turned to the book with an amused smile. Finally, the covers closed and his balding stout body came alive with the story of the Donkey and the Cabbages.

When the storytelling ended, Harry took a hickory nut from the basket beneath his chair. He cracked it and stomped the floor for Anna to come. She crawled down out of her father's lap and toddled to him.

'Thumb-out,' he said, then fed her a tiny morsel of nutmeat.

'Next for me,' Veve said. She tipped her head back, squeezed her eyes, and widened her mouth, pretending to look like little Anna.

"Thumb-out,' Harry teased.

Chapter 11

Harry's Joke

Harry rose as the gray light of morning tiptoed across his bed. He prickled with excitement. This morning they were going to the cider mill to press apples. The Muncy schoolhouse was very near the mill, and with any luck he'd at least have a chance to peek in and wave hello to his hearing friends. He couldn't wait to see their astonished faces.

Out the window a dense fog rested on the Pennsylvania farmlands, rolling down between the hills like puffy mounds of freshly shorn sheep's wool. His father strode from the mist toward the barn. He had been to the orchards to check his trees. He checked them first thing every morning like an anxious parent.

But then maybe that's why his apples are so good, Harry thought. His father was one of the few Mr. Russell let pay in cider for pressing his apples. The rest had to pay cash, a cent and a half a gallon.

Harry waved from his high perch but his father didn't see him.

Through the floorboards he felt footsteps behind him. It was Ray. 'Mother say must hurry. Dress. Eat. Father angry i-f wait long,' Ray said. Harry reached right away for the trousers that hung on his bedpost.

Over breakfast his father cautioned the children to keep their hands low when they signed in town. 'Like-this.' He motioned in small gestures at his side. Harry's father looked directly at him. 'Understand?'

Harry nodded out of habit. They were the same instructions his father always gave.

Harry left the table, having barely touched his plate, and ran with the others to help hitch the wagon. The day before they had loaded it with sacks of apples and an empty cider barrel. Veve led the roan out of his stall and she and Harry held him still while Ray fastened the harness. Ray drove to the house, then they hopped over the seat and scrambled for places among the bags.

Climbing aboard, Harry's mother handed him a napkin folded around two biscuits. 'Eat very little. Must calm-down. Not want thin — ' She drew a long bean with her fingers. Harry grinned and accepted the sweet-smelling rolls thankfully.

The reins slapped the horse and they were off. Down into the fog they drove, over the bumpy lane, between the two large piles of stones marking the entrance to the farm, and off the lane onto a wider, rutted road. Then they started a long ascent out of the gauze air.

As usual, Harry's father was wearing his broad-rimmed felt hat. With the hat and the fringe of ashen hair hanging below, it was hard to tell he was bald. Harry leaned out over the side behind him to see, straining for a particular tree or a gully he knew. On an occasional curve he caught a glimpse of the horse's red flanks glistening in the moist morning. His father urged the horse to move faster, but Whoa would not be hurried.

Perhaps Whoa really was a suitable name, Harry smiled. He realized he'd forgotten to tell Ray about it. His sisters and brother sat facing backward toward the road they left behind. He tugged Ray's shirt sleeve.

'What want?' Ray answered.

'That horse have name?'

'No. J-u-s-t call Horse.'

'I have name for,' Harry said.

'What?'

'W-h-o-a.'

Ray wrinkled his nose. 'Silly. Where find that name?'

'Can't tell now. Wait. Big surprise. Will show-you.' Harry gloated, but Ray looked crosser by the minute, waiting for something to happen. 'After-while. Can't now,' Harry said when Ray nagged him to see the surprise now.

Ray gestured, 'Bah. Can't believe you. You make fun. Not any surprise.' He folded his arms and stared out the back of the wagon.

'You see,' Harry retorted.

They were coming to a level place in the road. Harry pursed his lips. His throat vibrated a little, then more, and stopped. He waited, every muscle taut.

The roan continued his lumbering pace.

Harry looked in disbelief. Holding his throat this time, he gave a big push from deep in his stomach. He could feel a powerful burst spread through his chest and throat. He lowered his hand and wished for a lurch. Whoa slowed to a standstill and nibbled the tall grasses by the side of the road.

When Ray turned around, startled, Harry smiled knowingly at him, but Ray didn't seem to grasp what had happened.

'Why make stop?' said Harry's mother.

Harry's father shrugged. 'Not,' he answered. 'Horse. Self.'

'Maybe horse tired. Steep-hill, many people and many apples. Hard work pull. Rest.'

Harry's father agreed with his wife's suggestion and let the animal rest for a few minutes, but he soon was impatient with the wait and started up again. Harry sat solemnly; inside he danced with merriment.

The wagon bounced steadily, up and down hills, in and out of the fog. Reaching a hilltop they burst upon the sun and later waded into patches of thinning moisture. The farther they rode, the itchier Harry became to try his trick again. The fog was beginning to burn off and he could see a clearing ahead.

Now! He rounded his mouth and once again felt a mighty eruption in his chest. His heart pounded. A few beats later Whoa pulled to a stop.

Harry's parents glanced uneasily at each other. His father climbed down from his seat. He patted the horse and brushed his hand over the velvety rump. He examined the animal's mouth. The bit was in place. He signed to his wife. 'Horse not look tired.'

'Look-at shoes. Maybe losing one.'

'Good idea.' Harry's father lifted each hoof and studied it, while Whoa waited patiently. No, Harry's father shook his head. He wiped his forehead and looked the roan over once more. As he walked back to the wagon, Harry ducked behind the seat.

Whoa started the wagon rolling. Up front the two

adults puzzled over the strange behavior of their horse. Harry's father touched two fingers to his nose. 'Something funny.'

'Why you laugh?' Ray said to Harry.

'I d-o.'

'What?'

'Stop horse.'

'You? No. Can't believe. Lazy horse, that's-all.'

'I yell.'

'Yell?'

'Yes. School teach-me. Watch.'

Past the clearing was a small stand of evergreens, then there were a few farms and another turnoff onto a dusty road that followed the river like a weary companion into Muncy. The river road often was crowded with other vehicles. Harry calculated he had one more chance.

For the third time, he took a deep breath and he could feel the yell escaping. For the third time Whoa stalled.

'You d-o?' Ray's eyes goggled. Harry smirked.

The wagon had barely come to rest when their father jumped down, ripped off his hat, and snapped it against a wheel. Whoa pawed the ground. Again his father painstakingly examined the horse, his mouth, the shoes, the harness. Then he examined the wagon wheels and the axles. 'Nothing wrong,' he signed to himself.

Then one by one he fixed his gaze on the children draped over the side. A smile tugged at Harry's mouth, and he tried not to look for too long.

Thinking and in slow motion, Harry's father mounted his seat. He turned deliberately to Harry. His right hand crashed to his left palm. 'Stop! No-more! You think funny, you can stay. Get-off wagon. Off! Wait here.'

Harry was stunned. He crawled over his brother and sisters — Veve was near tears and Ray was pale with fright — and dangled a moment at the end of the cart before he dropped to the dirt road. As the wagon pulled off, his mother was signing to his father, but he ignored her protests. Whoa rounded the corner and disappeared.

Harry walked to a nearby fence post and drooped against the rough wood. He felt lost, though it was a place he knew well.

The morning fog was completely gone now. The sun was full and the sky glowed blue. In a few minutes they'd be at the cider mill. He kicked the dirt, covering the toes of his shoes with dust.

Soon a wagon appeared on the main road and his hopes leapt. Maybe they would give him a ride to town. He cut himself short. No, they were hearing for sure. That would anger his father more. He picked up a fistful of pebbles and threw them at the fence post.

Probably Ray was on his way to the schoolhouse already. Or the bridge.

He stuck his hands in a coat pocket and pulled out the rolls. Maybe if he ate he'd feel better. He broke off a hunk of roll. The roll was dry and stuck in his throat like the bitterness he felt.

He scuffed his shoes again. He wasn't going to wait here forever with nothing to do. He'd walk, he resolved. But to Muncy? Or home?

He turned his back on the river road and started out at a moderate and constant pace, the way his father had showed him to hike on the farm without overtiring himself. Avoiding the deep ruts, he strode past one farm. Then another.

The air was cool, but the sun was hot. Soon his undershirt was damp and clung to his body. He removed his coat and tied it around his waist. The dry, parched feeling in his mouth was becoming more insistent. He hesitated at the next farmhouse, thinking of asking for a drink of water, then decided against it.

After a while, he reached the stand of trees near the clearing where he had stopped Whoa the second time. He shinnied up the tallest tree like a fleeing chipmunk. On one side he saw the rough up-and-downhill trek ahead of him. On the other, he saw how far he'd come. The river road was barely visible.

Then in the distance he noticed movement on the road. He recognized it as his parents. He could see his father pull up the wagon and get out, probably near the place where he left Harry. They were looking for him.

For a long time — it seemed like hours — his father just stood there. At last he climbed back into the wagon. Harry was astounded by what he saw next. The wagon turned in at each farm and drove up to the farmhouse. After a few minutes they were on the rough dirt road again, rolling very slowly closer and closer to him.

As the wagon approached, he could see his family's worried expressions. Even Anna was searching the road for some trace of her brother. But no one glanced up, so no one spied him. The wagon inched along.

Harry wanted to fly down from his hiding place but an angry part of him held back. He twisted from the right to the left of the tree trunk to get a better view. They were directly beneath him. Now moving away. Soon they would be gone.

Harry held tightly to the tree and drew up his lips. With all the strength he could summon he pushed out the biggest "Whoa!" he'd ever made.

The horse jerked short. Immediately, Harry's father

stood up in the wagon and looked about. 'Come-back,' he said with a generous motion that even hearing would know as a welcome.

Harry clambered down out of the tree so fast he skipped the lower branches entirely. He pressed hard against his father.

His father patted his blond hair, then lifted his chin gently. 'You much like father. Stubborn.' A wrinkle creased the corners of his mouth. He removed his felt hat and pulled it over Harry's ears. 'Come. Better wear coat. Riding not warm like walking. B-a-c-k to apple mash house. Not finished.'

Harry ran to the rear of the wagon where Ray moved over to make room for him. The wagon started up. 'You right,' Ray remarked shyly to Harry, their shoes trailing in the dust billows, 'true surprise.'

Chapter 12

Reunion

Muncy was not elegant, spacious Philadelphia. The streets were dusty and unpaved. Buildings had settled unevenly. Front porches butted too close to the walkways and added-on rooms hung like stiff broken limbs. Yet as they drove through town Harry felt at home. The worn buildings and parched streets were old friends.

Occasionally someone on foot looked up and waved a greeting or a dog ran alongside, nipping at the wagon wheels. They were rolling past the Grange Hall and Harry asked his father, 'W-h-e-n f-a-i-r?' Each year, usually in November or December, the villagers gathered at the hall for a last burst of fun before they took leave of each other and burrowed in for the winter. There were contests and dancing. Harry's mouth watered when he thought of the food. He hoped he hadn't missed it.

'Soon,' his father answered.

'Before go-back school?' Yes, his father nodded. 'Can go?' Yes again, he nodded. Harry clapped gleefully.

When they arrived at the cider mill, only one other wagon was pulled up outside. The same sign still glared from the tree next to the hitching rail: ROTTEN APPLES MAKE ROTTEN CIDER. At the peak of the season cider making often meant several hours' wait, but Mr. Russell wasn't the kind to hurry his customers through and throw all the apples together. Every farmer's cider was pressed from his own apples.

Harry, Veve, and Ray started unloading the fruit while their father went inside. The mill owner soon stepped out with his eldest son. He winked at the baby, who was hiding behind a sack. She covered her eyes and Mr. Russell laughed.

He reached in a bag and bit into an apple. As he chewed, pleasure rippled over his face. He took out a piece of paper and scribbled something for Harry's father. His father read the note and relaxed visibly. Then Mr. Russell pointed to Harry and Ray. His father shook his head and took the pencil. He wrote a few words. Mr. Russell smiled again. He spoke to his son, who started helping with unloading the wagon, and left with a backward wave.

'What man say?' Harry's mother asked.

'Said l-u-c-k-y I have two sons. Will have two more good apple farmers. I tell-him second son go-away to school, but my girl good farmer. Right?' Harry's father looked to Veve.

Veve's head bobbed and she attacked the apple pile eagerly. Harry's father watched, bemused. 'Easy,' he cautioned. 'Hurry, quick become tired.'

When the wagon was unloaded, Harry's mother asked him to run an errand for her while she shopped at the general store. 'Take dress for M-r-s. P-o-o-l-e.' She handed Harry a parcel on a pair of strings. 'And ask i-f more sewing.'

'May ride horse?'

Harry's father rubbed his chin. 'Why need horse?'

Harry knew his father guessed what he was up to. 'Maybe looking-around.' He was lying only a little. If he didn't find his friends, he intended to browse.

'Boy enjoy looking. Not see here long time,' his mother interjected.

His father softened. 'O-K. But not much long. Maybe apples finish fast.'

Harry signaled for Ray to come along. They detoured Whoa past the schoolhouse, but it was empty. 'Maybe hearing same my school,' Harry explained as they peered in the dark window. 'No school Saturday afternoon. Only morning.'

Mrs. Poole lived in one of the few houses set away from the road. Ray held Whoa and kept an eye out for Freckles. Harry rapped at the door, and a few moments later a strange woman, not Mrs. Poole, pushed the door open. Harry showed her the package and pointed to the name neatly inscribed on the wrapping. The door swung closed and Harry was about to turn away when it yawned once more and revealed a beaming Mrs. Poole.

Mrs. Poole bent forward to receive her parcel and a sweet smell of honeysuckle bent with her, caressing Harry's face. She handed a second package to him, tucked several coins into his coat pocket, and pressed another firm, round piece into his mitten. She pointed to the coin, then pointed to Harry. Again she pointed. Harry understood. The money in his pocket was for his mother; the money in his mitten was for him. His fingertips touched his lower lip. 'Thank-you.' Mrs. Poole's mouth parted and she disappeared behind the door.

Harry ran down the path to his brother, swinging Mrs. Poole's mending. 'Lady give money! We buy candy!'

They were just tying Whoa in front of the general store when Harry spied a familiar figure kicking stones in his direction. Freckles! The two boys ran for each other and there erupted a joyful dance of back pounding, hugs, leaps, and handshakes. Harry paused and feasted his eyes. He saw the same red hair. And the same flecks clung to the bridge of his friend's nose. He still reminded him of a bran muffin.

Harry removed his mitten and touched his fingertips to his face. 'Freckles.'

Freckles pointed to Harry, then twisted his fist at the corner of his mouth, 'You Apple.' And the boys broke into another round of shoving and jumping.

Harry formed several more signs. 'School far. That why see nothing long time. Vacation now.' Freckles answered with a puzzled expression. Harry said it again, slowly. 'School.' His hand whisked the air. 'Far.' He mimed reading and writing.

Freckles smiled blandly. 'You Apple,' he signed once more.

Harry felt a brief nettle of disappointment. But then Freckles gestured for him to follow. Mrs. Poole's package was left dangling on the horse and he and Ray ran after their hearing friend.

Around the wheelwright's, past the general store, behind the livery stable they played. The game of chase gave way to hide-and-seek.

'Now you,' said Harry to his brother. Ray and Freckles scurried away. He waited for them to get a head start, then dropped beside a horse tied to a hitching post and sidled to the next corner of a fence, alert for a shadow or flicker.

He was crouched beside a tree when all at once Freckles tagged him from behind. Harry jumped. 'Scare-me!' he exclaimed.

When they tired of hide-and-seek, the three boys unhitched Whoa and rode down to the old bridge. They meandered between trees, hopping off and on Whoa to collect sweet-gum nuts and beechnuts until their pockets bulged.

They sprawled on the riverbank and sorted through their nuts. The broken ones they threw into the stream.

Harry tapped Freckles and, using a small twig, inscribed the letter A in the hard dirt and pointed to his right hand, which looked like a fist. He wrote B and his hand stood upright, the letter C and his fingers curved. Harry pointed to the A and to Freckles. 'You. You. A.'

Freckles stuck up a hand and imitated Harry's A and the B.

'G-o-o-d,' Harry fingerspelled and wrote on the ground. He gestured to each letter of the word and coaxed Freckles to follow. Ray smiled at Freckles's G and rearranged the fingers. O came easily. On D Freckles fumbled. At last his hand obeyed.

Harry warmed with pleasure. His friend was re-membering.

Suddenly Freckles looked around. Something in the distance had caught his attention. He ran up the river bank a way and soon two other boys climbed over the crest of the slope. Harry recognized them both.

Freckles huddled with the newcomers. He glanced at Harry and the others looked his way, too. Mouths flapping, smiling, they came over to him. Ray hung back and fiddled with Whoa.

'Hi,' Harry saluted. The boys returned the greeting.

Freckles touched the dirt alphabet and waggled his finger at Harry, at each of the other boys, and at himself.

Harry motioned to Ray. 'What think want?'

'Think maybe want learn sign-language?' Ray asked in return.

Harry's grin widened. 'That what I think.' He pointed two fingers at himself like two eyes. 'Watch-me.' He tapped with his toe at the word spelled in the dirt and, bringing fingertips down from his mouth against his palm, signed, 'Good. Good. Good.' He molded Freckles's hands to approximate the sign.

Freckles removed his hands and shook his head no-no. He pointed to A-B-C and to himself.

'Signs better,' Harry gestured. 'More fast.' He turned to Ray again. 'Funny. Want only spelling.'

'Maybe spelling better for hearing,' Ray said. 'Many signs. Hard remember all.'

'Maybe.' Harry still was puzzled. When he taught Freckles before, Freckles had been interested in signs, too. Harry eyed his friend and the others curiously; then he plunged into his work.

He held up his hands for them to copy. After he and Ray fixed their fingers, they proceeded to the next letter, and the next. Sometimes fingers jutted every which way and the boys squirmed, but Harry urged them on. 'Good. Good.' On a second pass through the alphabet Freckles was doing well, but the other two missed so many that Harry tried sketching little diagrams to help them. In the pebbles and stiff earth they looked little better than Anna's scratchings.

Then Freckles took his friends aside. Harry tried unsuccessfully to ferret some meaning out of their lips. Only their eyes talked to him. They were excited. That much he could sense.

Freckles commandeered Whoa, took Harry and Ray by the arm, and the five of them walked side by side in the direction of town. Happy to be moving again and spirits raised, Harry felt like showing off. He drew himself up and recited: "Shoes. Salt. Girls."

The three boys turned to him. They looked startled.

'What happen?' said Ray.

Harry's lips curled in a smile. 'I talk.' Then they

laughed, even Ray. Freckles clapped him on the back and urged him to do it again and he obliged. He knew they were laughing at the way he must sound, but he didn't care.

They came upon the railroad line leading into Muncy. The hearing boys followed the tracks, balancing on the steel rails. Ray refused to walk with them. 'Dangerous for deaf,' he scolded Harry. 'Father teach us never near train.' For a time Harry stayed close to Ray, but his caution was short-lived and he joined the others jumping over the wood ties, while Ray glowered.

In town they stopped at a white frame building not far from Mrs. Poole's. It looked like the other houses on the street, graying and misshapen. Harry knew it was Freckles's house. He'd stood outside searching for his friend many times before, but he'd never been invited inside. Freckles opened the door and waved them on in. The other hearing boys dropped their coats and mittens in the dark coatroom off the kitchen and moved into the light. Harry churned with curiosity. He poked Ray to go in.

A clock, its face carved to look like the man in the moon, caught his attention. Suddenly its eyes rolled from side to side. 'Look!' Harry waved to Ray.

Meanwhile, Freckles brought out paper and pencil. He urged them on Harry. Harry wasn't sure what to do. Freckles took the pencil and wrote: "A-B-C. Can you draw the pictures?" He fingerspelled the same letters.

'O-o-o,' Harry's mouth pursed. He penciled a thin hand formed to read A, a second to read B. He showed the paper to Freckles. Yes, yes, Freckles nodded.

The three boys crowded around as he carefully drew the remaining hand positions. Freckles spelled the alphabet using the piece of paper. The other two wrenched the drawings away from him and tried too.

Harry clasped his hands together and held them high. 'Congratulations.'

The clock eyes rolled again. 'Late. Better go,' Ray pleaded.

Freckles went with them to the back door. He held the paper. 'T-h-a-n-k y-o-u,' he spelled.

Harry and Ray headed for the cider mill. Harry thought about Freckles with the piece of paper. He was feeling very pleased with himself. 'Think maybe not become tailor. Maybe teacher,' he said to his brother. Ray didn't reply. A teacher like Mr. Bertie, Harry dreamed.

Chapter 13

Preacher Ervin

A heavy stomp rippled through the wide planking to the table where Harry sat drawing. His hand shook and ink dribbled from his pen, leaving two coal-black eyes in the middle of his sketch. His mother stood in the doorway, a laundry basket in her arms. Her face was flushed, as if she had run very fast to the farm-house.

'What?' Harry frowned.

'Preacher coming. Tell children wash and comb. Now.'

'Hooray!' Harry clapped. He whisked his drawing tools from the table and ran to fetch the others. He found Veve and Anna rolling down a hillock and Ray in the barn sweeping out cow stalls. They broke off what they were doing and hurried after him to the kitchen.

Harry scrubbed his face and hands at the pump and slicked his hair. He grabbed his coat and, once out the door, flung his arms wide and plunged downhill.

Their visitor turned in at the stone pillars and plodded toward the pond. When he saw Harry he raised his arm and described a slow arc over his hat. Harry answered with a similar greeting. They quickly reached signing distance of each other. Harry's feet slowed and his hands picked up the running gait. 'Happy see-you! Mother see first. But I talk first!'

Preacher Ervin's tanned cheeks rose above his heavy black beard. 'Yes. Yes.' He continued toward Harry, his old horse shifting beneath him, side to side. 'You look happy. School suits you?' he said.

Now the signs tumbled from Harry's fingers like water chasing over rocks, too fast for beginnings or endings.

'Take time. Please. My eyes old. Lazy. Drink-in slow same turtle walks,' Preacher Ervin teased. He stretched himself to full height as though he were astride a pulpit. 'First I see, your signs strangers. I visit many deaf. All sign different. Some use large signs. Some small.' Mr. Ervin's nose and eyebrows pinched together to show how small. 'Sometimes my eyes walk. Comfortable. Sometimes eyes must run-

run-run. Still not understand. When I leave, your hands and my eyes will-be good friends.' He winked, relaxing his stiff posture.

'My eyes never forget your hands!'

The minister laughed and extended an arm to help lift Harry in front of him. Harry raised his hands so Mr. Ervin could see and he started his story again — pausing between football and pillow fights and Landis.

Harry was describing their new horse when his brother and sisters crowded around. Mr. Ervin swung off his mount and boosted each one behind Harry.

Their mother was waiting for them at the top of the hill. The wisps of long brown hair that minutes ago hung in a tangle over her forehead and at the nape of her neck were neatly folded and tucked away. She wore a clean apron and her eyes and cheeks radiated. She clasped Preacher Ervin's hand in her two and held it. 'Apple tell-you about school?'

'Yes.' He smiled. 'But much fast.'

'We worry, worry, but you right,' she said.

'My work for help,' Mr. Ervin replied.

Harry's mother led the preacher to the farmhouse. The kitchen was a rich coffer of smells. Traces of yesterday's dark bread mingled with the sweet aroma of carrots and onions and of brewing coffee. Harry's father came downstairs. He'd changed into a clean shirt and suspenders instead of his usual coveralls. He and Mr. Ervin greeted each other warmly. Preacher Ervin sat at the head of the table and everyone gathered around.

Harry watched expectantly. He didn't want to miss a wrinkled brow or a toss of the wrist. Then Mr. Ervin's hands unfurled with the news, tidbits of happenings he'd collected from deaf people in one little town or another. Most of the people Mr. Ervin mentioned Harry had never met, but he knew them and details of their family life as certainly as if they were neighbors.

Harry sucked in his breath quickly when he learned Mr. Titus's boy had lost a finger chopping wood. 'O-w-w-w,' he shook his hand.

'Mrs. Runkle soon another baby. Spring,' said Mr. Ervin.

'Hope she get girl,' Harry's mother said. 'Five boys. Terrible many. Me l-u-c-k-y. Have two boys. Two girls. Each has one brother and one sister.' She stopped. 'But she has more l-u-c-k than me in one thing. Her boys can hear. First, I hope for her hearing baby. Second, girl.'

'Mr. Runkle finish building new barn?' Harry's father tapped his elbow for Mr. Runkle's sign-name.

'Better hurry,' his mother winked at Mr. Ervin. 'Need sleep-room for new baby. Same baby Jesus.'

The minister smiled and scratched his beard. He

went on. Elizabeth English, the Englishes' eldest
daughter who they thought was hearing, was probably a deaf mute, too. And recently he married a deaf
couple in Scranton, he told them.

Now it was Harry's family's turn to replenish his
supply of news. 'What can I carry about you?' the
preacher asked, singling out Harry. 'About p-i-l-l-o-w
fights at deaf school?'

Harry reddened. 'No. Silly. Tell Jim Titus sorry
about finger. Tell-him I look for-him at deaf school.
Think Jim start school?'

'Maybe next-year. Hard for his father without. Need
Jim for work on farm,' the preacher said. Harry's father
shook his head sympathetically.

'Not hard for-you,' Harry said to his father.

'Yes. Sometimes,' he answered solemnly.

Harry was surprised. 'You have Ray.'

'True. But mother and I sad for our son. Children
sad for their brother.'

Harry was taken aback. It hadn't occurred to him
his leaving home was painful to them, too. 'Better
hearing,' he said. 'Can stay home. Walk to school.
Still help farm.'

'No, no,' his mother interrupted. 'Long walk to
M-u-n-c-y.' She overdrew the sign for long. 'Your
school better. Short walk. Up-down stairs, your
school.' Everyone laughed. 'Tell about learning cloth-

ing,' his mother suggested after the gaiety subsided. 'Mr. and Mrs. English and Titus never go school. Interesting for them.'

'Good idea.' Harry launched into an enthusiastic description. He rubbed his fingers together to show the fine feel of the wools they used. He pumped his feet to show how the treadle machine operated. His hands traced its steady shiver. 'Round-round-round.' His cheeks billowed telling about the steam-filled pressing room. His father raised his eyebrows when Harry reached the part about his drawings and just how he was changed from the printing to the tailoring shop. 'Drawing best. Enjoy most.'

He paused and considered what he was going to say next. 'Sometimes think maybe I want teach deaf, myself. In-future. Notice not one deaf teacher my school.'

'You?' Preacher Ervin looked positively startled, then grinned as if the thought were wonderfully funny. 'Much sun on head. Dizzy. Must talk i-f want teach. How can deaf? Hearing best teacher.' His hand sliced the air, meaning finished, nothing more to say.

Harry wanted to argue, but he felt weak under Mr. Ervin's pronouncement. It was as if someone had cut off his wind. He looked to his father, who shifted in his seat, but his stolid expression gave no hint of what he was thinking. Harry's uneasiness grew.

Finally it was his mother who responded. 'Think depend on what teach. Some things much talking, yes, must hearing. But i-f teach carpentry, maybe drawing, small difference.'

'I-m-p-o-s-s-i-b-l-e,' Preacher Ervin protested. But Harry's mother was no longer watching. She rose and busied herself around the table, clearing coffee mugs and putting out utensils. She kept her eyes down to avoid Mr. Ervin, while Mr. Ervin watched intently.

At last he turned away and patted Anna. 'Now your time tell preacher.' Anna cheerfully related a story about her cat catching a mouse and dropping it at her feet. Her chubby fingers, the little incomplete gestures, brought a smile and broke the tension.

Soon bowls of hot stew warmed the table. Preacher Ervin tore off a chunk of fresh bread, then handed each person a smaller piece. He stood and signed a blessing. Steam wafted from his dish — curling with the air currents his hands created — and disappeared among his whiskers.

How beautifully Mr. Ervin spoke, Harry thought, with magnificent swoops and swirls. These were church signs to please the eye, not everyday signs intended for speed. And how unlike Mr. Bertie's church, where the hearing sat stiff and restless all afternoon.

The news continued over their meal. Afterward, Mr. Ervin took down the Bible he had presented to the family long ago. He opened the book and propped it before him. The ornate signs reappeared. Graceful, unhurried, they told the story of Jesus healing the blind man.

Preacher Ervin closed the book and sat down. This was the part Harry liked best, when he could ask questions and think over the passage the preacher read for them. They held a lively discussion about miracles and afflictions, but Harry felt uneasy again when Preacher Ervin said God put some people on earth to suffer to remind the hearing and the seeing of their sins. Harry wondered. Suffer? He felt no pain. His ears did not hurt with the absence of sound.

That evening as he crawled into bed, Harry's mother came to his attic room, carrying a lamp. She fussed with an extra blanket. 'Begin cold nights,' she said. Harry knew she was looking for an excuse to talk.

He pulled his arms out from under the comforter. 'What you think hearing feel like?'

His mother stopped tucking in the blanket and sat beside him on the bed. 'I think same seeing. Feel nothing different. J-u-s-t see. Not think, think seeing. Hearing maybe same. Feel nothing. One hear, finish.'

He remembered the blind man walking alone on the Philadelphia streets with only a stick to guide him. 'Why preacher say deaf can't teach? You believe?'

His mother drew closer. 'Preacher good man. Help deaf many times. But not know everything about deaf people. Don't afraid. I-f you want teach deaf, must try. That's-all. Never know, i-f never try. In head must think can. Brave.'

'But why preacher say not?' Harry insisted.

'Sometimes hearing have funny ways,' she said. Harry smiled. That was her explanation for anything the hearing did she didn't like. She hugged him and said, 'You teacher, I become very proud,' and she wiggled like a fancy bird fluffing its feathers. Harry laughed and turned over.

In the morning Harry watched Preacher Ervin as his horse picked its way carefully down the slope. Usually Harry accompanied the other children with him to the pond. Today he stood beside his mother and waved from the top of the hill.

Chapter 14

At the Fair

Harry mounted the Grange steps two at a time and slipped between several people to the meeting room. Red and white bunting ruffled along the walls. The tables were laden with towers of preserves, canned goods, and fancy sewing. The clean smell of evergreen boughs decorating the doorway mingled with the hot aroma of mulled cider and fresh doughnuts.

People were everywhere. A rosy-cheeked man and woman stood at attention in front of a photographer's leggy black box. Then they threw their heads back, laughing, as if to shake off the picture pose. A gentleman wearing a blue ribbon on his lapel paused before a pyramid of apples. He selected one, pressed and tapped it near his ear, and replaced it with as much care as if it were an egg. Here and there grownups too

old to stand sat on clusters of folding chairs beside
children with legs too short to reach the floor.

Harry read the placard near the entrance: MAGIC
SHOW — 2:00 P.M., SPELL-DOWN — 3:00 P.M., JUDGING
RESULTS — 5:00 P.M., DANCING — ALL EVENING.

He felt a tap on his shoulder and started to step
aside. It was his father. 'Look for you. Help bring
things inside,' he signed discreetly. Harry nodded and
followed his father out to the wagon. He and Ray
hoisted the keg of cider up on his father's back and
guided him through the crowd hovering at the entrance, which parted obligingly, and inside the hall
to their usual places at the end table. Then they went
back for baskets of Winesaps, zucchini relish, and the
stools. When they had delivered the horse and wagon
to the stable, Harry was free to roam the fair.

He looked for where the children were congregated.
He knew that was the most exciting place to be. Next
to the stage he discovered a group of them crouched
around a crank-operated machine. He edged closer.
They were peering one at a time into a whirring cylinder. From time to time a woman stopped the handle, reached inside and removed a long slip of paper
with markings on it, and substituted a new paper. One
boy stood over the cylinder too long and two older
fellows pried him off.

Finally Harry clutched the handle and wound it

furiously as he'd seen the others do. At first the markings blurred together, but soon the lines seemed to
lift from the paper and move in harmony. He saw a
miniature sun rise and fall. The woman inserted a second paper. This time a stick figure juggled several
balls. On the third reel a lion tamer snapped his whip
at a lion. Up, down, the tip of the whip flicked while
the lion's mouth opened and closed in answer.

Harry skirted the crowd back to their table to tell
Ray about the wonderful picture machine. But when
he arrived, Ray was nowhere to be seen and he could
tell by his father's posture that the apple judging was
in progress.

His father's mouth was set in a hard smile, his limbs
taut. His mother, on the other hand, was loose and
eager. She watched the five men and women at the
next table openly. She jabbed Harry's father. 'Their
apples medium.'

The judges approached them and Harry's mother
squirmed with excitement as she offered the tin cup.
The examiners swirled and tipped the cider, and they
hefted, sniffed, and chewed the apples. Then they
made mysterious marks in their books. An elderly
woman wearing a wide-brimmed hat, nearly big
enough to topple her, stepped closer to Harry's parents — his mother first — and graciously squeezed a

hand. She said something framed in her thin lips. It was friendly, maybe congratulatory.

At last the judges left, and Harry's mother swept Anna and Veve in a dancing embrace.

'Win?' Veve asked.

'Maybe not first. But feel certain win ribbon,' she boasted. Harry loved it when his mother acted so sure of herself. It made him feel stubborn and proud, too.

People were gathering at the other end of the hall. 'Go,' Harry's mother motioned to them. 'Take children. Time for m-a-g-i-c. I watch here. Where Ray?'

Ray stepped out of the milling crowd as if he'd been waiting for her to ask. 'Hey,' he waved to Harry, 'saw funny —' and he cranked his arm in a circle.

'I know. Saw already.'

Harry's father stood at the back of the audience with Anna perched on his shoulders, while Harry and Ray led Veve in and around the grownups to the front. Harry spotted Freckles. He waved but Freckles was busy talking. He made a path to his friend. 'H-e-l-l-o,' he fingerspelled.

Freckles looked a little embarrassed. He fidgeted, then answered. 'H-e-l-l-o H-a-r-r-y.'

Harry felt enormously pleased. 'You p-r-a-c-t-i-c-e-d. S-p-e-l-l-i-n-g p-e-r-f-e-c-t.' Freckles blushed again. Harry continued, signing the words he thought

Freckles could grasp easily, spelling those he didn't. 'S-o-o-n I go-away. To school.' He repeated. 'S-c-h-o-o-l.' Freckles caught his meaning. He nodded. 'S-o-r-r-y w-i-l-l n-o-t s-e-e you. L-o-n-g,' Harry spelled.

Freckles nodded again and abruptly looked away, pretending to be intent on the stage. The stage was empty. Harry tapped Freckles. 'G-o-o-d-b-y-e,' he said and left to find Veve and Ray. Later he glanced back at Freckles over the heads of the children. He'd been so strange, almost unfriendly, with him.

But he quickly forgot Freckles. A man wearing a tall top hat and a black cape lined in shimmering red fabric, and carrying a black stick, climbed onto the stage. Under the hat Harry recognized the shopkeeper of the general store. The man swept his cape and minced from side to side. The black and red garment unfurled and he pulled out a nosegay, which he tossed to the audience. Harry stretched for the flowers but they sailed well over his head.

The cape whirled again. Out came a chicken. Harry laughed. The robe furled. The chicken disappeared. He looked for a telltale bulge. He couldn't find one anywhere.

When the card tricks started, Harry lost interest. He looked around at the other children. Suddenly they were squeezing their faces in surprise. The chicken was flapping through a shower of cards. That chicken again, Harry laughed.

The magician approached the edge of the stage. The children around them were waving their hands frantically, so Harry and Ray and Veve did the same. The magician pointed to Harry. Harry glanced backward to his father, who was signing 'No.' Harry let the man walk him to center stage.

The cape whirled before his face and a long strand of scarves — red, yellow, blue, green — escaped from the tip of the baton. Another flourish and the scarves disappeared. The magician held the cape in front of Harry's face again. It seemed forever when the cape finally dropped. Harry looked for his father at the perimeter of the crowd. He was still glowering. Now he was laughing.

Harry twisted to see behind him, but the magician directed his head forward. Out of the corner of his eye he watched the scarves. They were coming from his head. They were coming from his shirt collar, his sleeve, his pants pocket. A long train of colored cloths lay in a pile at his feet. And still the magician was pulling out scarves.

Now he placed the tall hat over Harry's ears. All Harry could see was his feet. Two hands were guiding him slowly off the stage when he felt something warm moving inside the hat. It had hard skinny claws. What-ever it was, it was digging into his hair. Harry reached up to yank off the hat — and out flew the chicken!

The magician opened his mouth wide with aston-ishment and reached under the bird. He held out a smooth brown egg for Harry. The audience clapped and grinned.

Harry climbed down off the stage and the children crowded around to examine his egg. A couple of them wanted to hold it, Harry could tell, but he wouldn't let it out of his hands.

Soon the excitement died and he was left by him-self. Even Ray wandered off. He wadded his handker-chief in the bottom of his shirt pocket and carefully placed his egg inside.

He cast about the hall for some new excitement. He couldn't wait for the dancing — lines of people spin-ning and stepping in unison. Sometimes he and Ray tried a swing or two in a corner. But the dancing wasn't for hours yet.

People clustered near the stage again for the spell-down. He disliked the spell-downs — the hearing talked too much — but he was attracted to the crowd and he drifted around the edges waiting for something more interesting to catch his eye.

At the center of attention several boys and girls shifted nervously on risers. One by one they stepped down before the audience and recited. If the people clapped, they returned to the risers. If there was no clapping, they sat on the side. Gradually the numbers at the sides swelled, while the group on the risers dwindled.

One of the few remaining boys looked familiar. Harry moved forward. The boy came down off the riser and back another time. He was Freckles's friend, one of the fellows by the river the day Harry's family pressed apples.

Probably Freckles was somewhere in the crowd watching, too. Harry set out to find him. He circled the audience. At the very front beneath center stage he found Freckles's carrot-red hair.

Bending so he wouldn't block the people behind him, he pushed closer, working his way to the center. 'H-i a-g-a-i-n.' Harry beamed. Freckles ignored him. He tried once more. 'Your f-r-i-e-n-d w-i-n-n-i-n-g.'

Freckles seemed angry. His mouth clenched and his hand trembled. 'G-o a-w-a-y,' he spelled. Harry was stunned.

Freckles's friend left the risers. His turn was coming more often. He looked to the matron at his right, who spoke, and he looked down at Freckles. Then Harry saw Freckles hold his hand in front of his chest. No one behind would notice. His fingers were forming letters, 'N-i-n-t-h.' He spelled it again. 'N-i-n-t-h.'

Freckles's friend spoke. He smiled smugly and returned to his place in line.

Harry's stomach clenched like a fist. He pulled at
Freckles. 'C-h-e-a-t?'

'D-o-n-t t-e-l-l.' Freckles's face was so red the
blotches blurred and disappeared. Beads of perspira-
tion formed on his forehead.

Again the boy stepped before the woman. Harry
noticed the book in Freckles's lap for the first time.
Freckles flipped the pages hurriedly. 'A-r-g-u-m-e-n-t.
A-r-g-u-m-e-n-t,' he spelled.

Harry froze.

'D-o-n-t t-e-l-l.' Freckles put an arm around Harry,
cajoling.

Harry tried to smile, but he couldn't. He didn't want
to believe what was happening.

All of a sudden an arm reached down and snatched
the book from Freckles. A man with thick jowls shook
the book at the woman. The spell-down stopped. Soon
an official was pushing Freckles and Harry up to the
stage. Moments later someone collared Freckles's
friend. The man was still shaking the book. His jowls
flapped as his mouth shuttered rapidly. His heavy
brows knit in a fierce scowl.

Curiosity seekers pressed around them. Harry's father broke through, followed shortly by a woman
Harry knew was Freckles's mother.

'Tell-me!' his father demanded, making no attempt to conceal his signs. His father was angrier than Harry'd ever seen him.

Harry signed very small. 'Hearing boys cheat. Spelling. Use books and signs.'

'Whose fault? Yours.'

'No! No!' Harry protested.

His father exploded into a whirlwind. The people who were standing near drew away. 'Bad, much go-with hearing. Now you lie. Who teach signs? You! You help. Your responsibility. Now hearing stare-at us. Think all deaf cheat.'

Harry looked at the hearing surrounding them. Freckles's mother shot him an accusing gaze.

His father rummaged in his pockets. He found a piece of paper and pencil and scribbled something, which he showed to one of the judges, then turned to Harry. 'Wait outside for me. Must punish. Bad boy.'

Harry stared hard at Freckles. Freckles hung his head low. Harry turned and walked out of the meeting hall as he'd been ordered. He could feel the dozens of eyes trailing after him.

It was taking forever to reach the door. His head pounded with memories that flew at him like birds surrounding a cat. He saw his father again. Now hearing stare, his father had said. Now his mother. Silly, never afraid, she countered. Whoa, he yelled. Then

LeRoy came to him. You won and I lost, he said. No. The deaf won one and the hearing won one. They pounded and pounded inside his head.

Outside at last, he was surprised by the soothing cool air. He didn't care about the whipping he knew he'd get from his father. It was Freckles. A shudder crept between his shoulder blades. He wrapped his arms around himself, and he felt the lump in his pocket. He took out the egg and threw it on the ground.

He walked down the steps and continued straight ahead, faster and faster, first past the tree, past the stable, on past the train station. He pumped his legs still harder and he was running.

Chapter 15

Rescue

When Harry tired of running, he found himself at the old bridge. He stood on the slopes of the riverbank and picked up several stones. One by one he hurled them at the opposite shore. They dropped in the water. The last stone, caught on the wind perhaps, strained to reach, nearly crossing over, until it too fell short.

Harry shivered and blew into his hands. He'd left without a coat and the freezing air was biting at his skin. A lazy snowflake settled on his shirt sleeve. He couldn't stay out here indefinitely, he knew that.

He climbed the gentle crest and looked sadly on the old bridge, then headed toward town, taking the roundabout route. He shuffled alongside the railroad tracks. Once in a while he jumped the ties in awkward leaps. His legs were too cold to permit anything more graceful, but he felt better, warmer.

In the distance clouds were blotting out the last of the afternoon sun. It looked like snow, not just flurries. He quickened his pace.

Then around the bend, posted in the middle of the tracks, stood Freckles.

Freckles waved hello. He actually appeared happy to see him. Harry let him draw near, but instead of stopping, he shoved past and continued walking the tracks. Freckles loped beside him to keep up. His gestures begged him to wait. But Harry ignored them.

The next thing Harry felt was Freckles holding him by the shoulder and pulling him around. Harry raised his arm to throw off the grip and caught Freckles in the face. He sent him reeling. He hadn't intended to hit Freckles, but now that it was done, he wasn't sorry.

Freckles got up and rubbed his cheek and felt for the bridge of his nose, but he didn't come back at him.

Harry stalked off. He was aware of a second shadow, following close behind his. Sometimes the shadow gained upon him. Sometimes it dropped back. He pushed on stubbornly, flapping his arms to keep warm. He didn't care any more what Freckles did. He wasn't a friend. A true friend would never have humiliated him that way.

As they were nearing the outskirts of the village, he saw his father. He was looking into the dwindling sun, shielding his eyes. When his father saw him, he started in Harry's direction, shaking the coat he carried with him. Harry girded himself. He was ready to take his punishment.

Suddenly his father dropped the coat and he was running. He flailed, 'Away! Away!'

Bewildered, Harry stopped where he was. He started to look to his rear when he caught a flying leap to the ribs that knocked the air out of him. He catapulted sideways, rolling down the embankment with Freckles on top, then under, then on top of him. He rolled over once more to free himself of Freckles. In a fury he pounded on him.

Then through the ground came an unfamiliar, heavy rumble. A strong current of air rushed behind his head. He dropped his fist and turned. There on the embankment above, a freight train hurried over the same spot where he'd stood only moments before. He watched the cars roll by. He couldn't tear himself from the sight. The train was a long one: boxcar after boxcar, coal cars, and finally the caboose.

As the caboose glided past, he saw his father, who

scrambled around and down the gravel incline. He slid the last few feet and scooped Harry up and squeezed him. Over his shoulder Harry watched the last of the train.

His father held him a long time, rocking and swaying. When the embrace eased, round tears glinted on his round face. To Harry they seemed almost unnatural. He was hollow inside.

He looked around for Freckles. Freckles still lay on the ground with frightened eyes. His father stooped over him, picking off some of the pebbles and debris that clung to the boy's pants and coat; then he helped Freckles to his feet.

Freckles's mouth was a little swollen and dark red stained his nostrils. His father wagged his head. He took out a clean handkerchief and gently dabbed Freckles's nose and lips.

It was fast becoming too dark to sign. They started into town without trying to talk, pausing long enough to pick up Harry's coat. Harry walked on one side of his father and Freckles on the other. He studied Freckles's shoes and his own, dropping and lifting in the dusk. They were walking as if nothing had happened.

When they stopped outside the Grange hall in the light of a window, Harry's father rested his hand on

Freckles. 'Thank-you,' he signed. 'You save my son. Give many, many thanks.' Freckles scuffed at the dirt with his shoes. Harry's father turned to Harry. 'Think boy understand?'

'Some. Not all.'

His father reached for Freckles's hand. He pumped his wrist high. There could be no mistaking what he meant. Freckles grinned sheepishly. He faced Harry and looked as if he might try to say something but thought better of it. Instead, he raised his palm in a slight wave and skipped up the steps. Harry watched him disappear inside.

'Good boy,' his father said. 'Tell truth. Explain everything to hearing. About not your fault. His idea. We look for-you. Want tell-you.' His expression grew thoughtful. 'And brave boy,' he added. 'What boy's name?' he asked.

'Ray and I name-him Freckles,' Harry replied, using the sign-name. His father smiled.

Harry felt unnatural again. Here his father was smiling about Freckles and here he was not knowing what to feel. It was easier when his father openly disliked Freckles. 'Hearing two face,' Harry said.

His mother wept openly when she saw Harry. 'Waiting. Worry. Worry. Why gone so-long?' She clasped Harry tightly in the crook of her elbow as his father explained. 'Never train. Never!' she scolded, wiping her face. 'One thing deaf must always fear. Remember!'

'I know. I know.' Harry frowned. Right now he was impatient to forget about the train. Then he saw two blue ribbons on their table. 'Win?' he asked.

'Yes. One for apple drink. One for r-e-l-i-s-h,' his mother answered, but she didn't seem too interested. 'Think time go home. Tired. T-o-o much worry.'

'Stay. Short time,' Harry pleaded. 'Want see dancing.' The dancers were in formation already. 'Look,' he pointed.

'Baby tired,' his father said. Anna lay asleep huddled under the table on some coats.

'Please?'

Harry's mother glanced at his father. 'O-K. Little-bit.'

The dancers started up. They spun round and round like tops. They whirled in twos and fours with such sprightliness they moved in a blur of color. But the grandest sight was when all the dancers joined hands and circled the hall together. Harry grabbed up his mother's hand and Ray's and Veve's. They caught their father in the circle and twirled behind their table until they saw the hearing stop.

'Now go home,' Harry's mother said.

Harry knew she didn't really want to go. Her face

was flushed and she was enjoying herself again. 'One more dance?'

His mother winked. 'One.'

While they waited for the next dance to begin, Mrs. Poole visited at the table. She smiled sweetly and pointed out the ribbons and left, dangling a trail of scent behind her.

Veve held her nose. 'Strong smell. Whew,' she flapped her hand. Harry laughed. Veve was right.

One of the officials who had judged the apples stepped through the crowd of people. Harry had noticed him watching when they danced behind the table. He extended his arm to Harry's mother.

'What want?' she asked Harry's father.

The judge saw their exchange. He directed her attention to the couples lining up in two long rows. Harry's mother held back with a shy grin.

Harry's father said, 'Maybe i-f dance very good, give another blue ribbon.'

'You tease,' Harry's mother laughed. She slipped her arm in the judge's and he propelled her onto the dance floor. Harry was amazed at how smoothly she blended with the others. Each couple bowed and twirled and slid down the center between the rows of dancers. There was occasional confusion, but she copied what the other women did almost immediately.

'Mother good,' Harry remarked to his father.

'Smart woman,' he said. 'Watch others dancing. Know what d-o.' Then he added, 'Sometimes think your mother can hear little, but she say nothing.'

Harry was astonished. 'True?'

'Maybe.'

'I-f true, why mother not say anything?'

'Not-know. Sometimes think she not want make us feel bad.'

'You tell truth or playing?' His father grinned broadly. 'You fool me. You dreaming,' Harry complained. His father held him away with one hand and pretended to spar with the other. But the clowning was halfhearted and Harry wondered if his father knew for certain.

The judge was escorting his mother back. Harry watched her for some hint. 'Dizzy,' she puffed, when the judge left. 'First time. Make me feel light. Good fun.'

Harry's father poked around the collar of her dress, as if searching for something. 'What?' she asked.

'See no ribbon.'

'Go-on.' She shooed him away, pretending to be angry.

They packed their foodstuffs and stools during the next dance and drove home in the wagon soon after. The children curled in the back beneath the heavy horse blanket. But even with the blanket the cold stole under their wraps and they pushed closer together.

Harry watched the pinholes of light passing overhead as he rolled the day's happenings over and over in his mind. He could still see the man shaking the book and feel all those people watching him leave the hall in disgrace. The dull feeling had gone, replaced with the steady burn of resentment. He drew his arms tighter around Anna and Ray. If his mother could hear even a little, he thought, she was wise not to tell them.

Chapter 16

Good-byes

As he stood next to the kitchen stove pulling on his trousers and his shirt, Harry watched the trinkets on the Christmas tree slowly twist. This year his brother had carved a woolly lamb for Anna and hung it on a string near the bottom. His decoration was more fragile, so he placed it near the top. He had made a paper ballerina, putting her image on both sides of a thin sheet, and cut it out to look like the one he'd seen in the Philadelphia store window. She wore a short skirt and a wee crown and her arm reached in a gracious curve.

'Finish packing?' his mother asked. She was wearing the brooch with the shepherd and shepherdess.

'Yes. Yes.'

'Put-in new shirt I make for-you?'

'Yes. Finished. Everything.'

'Have bag apples for you bring to school. Some for you. Some for other boys. Hurry dressing. Soon leave. I-f late, no-more train until tomorrow.' His mother went back to working around the kitchen.

It made no difference, school or home. Someone was always telling him to hurry. He watched his mother sweep the floor. She moved briskly as if to catch the train with her broom.

'No dreaming,' she commanded.

Harry fastened the last button and stuck his nose in the fresh-smelling pine tree. He blew hard. The ballerina did a quick curtsy and leapt into a dizzying spin.

When they arrived at the train station, the trainmaster explained in a note to Harry's father that the train was late. According to a telegraph message, they were having problems many miles up the track. A switch was frozen. The train would be along, he wrote, as soon as they could fix the switch.

At first Harry felt as though he'd been given a reprieve, but after an hour and a half he paced the waiting room.

'Restless. Go-outside. Cool-air good for-you,' his mother said.

He stepped out the door into a swirl of giant snowflakes. He was rounding the corner of the station to the platform when he found Freckles and his two friends standing on benches peering into the waiting-room windows. It was as if the three boys were look-ing for him.

Harry felt confused. He nearly turned on his heels to go back inside, but something held him there. The boys raised their hands in greeting. He waved hello.

He continued out to the platform. The boys fol-lowed a few feet behind. He tried to look past them in the direction the train should be arriving. There was no sign of an engine. He tightened his muffler and pulled down the earflaps on his cap. The three boys stared up the tracks, too. Harry began wishing they would just go away.

At last Freckles came over to him. He took off a mitten and searched in his trousers pocket. He pulled out a yellow cat's eye. Harry admired the gleaming marble. It was gorgeous.

Freckles put out his hand to give it to him. Harry reacted almost with panic. He didn't want anything from him. No, no, he shook his head and pushed away the glass ball.

Freckles looked disappointed. He slipped the cat's eye back in his pocket and rummaged for something else. He got out his bag of marbles. Harry watched as he laid them in a circle on the platform. There were reds, greens, blues, and several milky white shooters.

Freckles beckoned to Harry. He was inviting him to join.

For a moment Harry didn't do anything. Then he squatted beside the circle. He fingered a marble. Yes, he'd play.

They fell easily into the game, like so many games they had played behind the general store. The boys lent Harry a shooter and later one to Ray and to Veve when they moved the game inside to escape the chill air.

The next hour passed rapidly and still the train did not come. The trainmaster shrugged and smiled.

Freckles indicated he should go home. Suddenly Harry felt the old anger welling. He caught Freckles's elbow and interrupted his marble collecting. He motioned, 'Follow-me.' He steered Freckles to a bench in a corner, where he wasted no time. 'W-h-y c-h-e-a-t?' he fingerspelled.

A deep red climbed Freckles's neck and cheeks, spilling over to the tips of his ear lobes. 'J-o-k-e,' he spelled.

'W-h-y?' Harry repeated.

Freckles scratched his head. He didn't answer.

'J-o-k-e o-n me? M-a-k-e f-u-n o-f me?' Harry persisted.

No, no. Freckles's head jerked violently. His hands flew up, trying to fingerspell, but they went lame and

143

made no sense. Freckles groped awkwardly. Then he noticed the windowpane. He blew on it. A white cloud covered the window.

Quickly he printed: "Thomas is a very bad speller." He pointed to the shorter of the two other boys. Harry followed the finger and nodded. He was the one in the contest. Freckles wiped the window with his sleeve. He blew. "We thought it would be very — " He wiped and blew again. "— funny if he won the spell-down."

'Oh,' Harry mouthed.

Freckles printed more. "I didn't think anyone would — find out. I'm very sorry." Freckles underlined the word *very*.

Harry studied the words on the window. He studied Freckles. He wanted to believe him. He looked away, trying to collect his thoughts. His mother was watching him. She made no attempt to sign, but he guessed what she would say anyway. Sometimes, the hearing have funny ways, he repeated for himself.

He fingerspelled to Freckles. 'F-r-i-e-n-d-s.' Then he signed the word, laying one index finger over the other and linking them as in a chain. 'Friends. You. Me. F-r-i-e-n-d-s. Friends.'

Freckles crossed his two fingers. 'Friends. You, Apple. Me, Friend,' he signed.

Harry laughed. 'No,' he signaled. 'Me Apple. You

Freckles.' He made invisible dots on his face. 'Apple
a-n-d Freckles friends.'

Freckles's face lit with understanding. 'You a-n-d
me friends.'

'Yes! Good.'

Harry saw his mother nodding. 'Proud. Not sour.
Make friends,' she signed in little gestures across the
room. He smiled.

Freckles shifted his gaze to the opposite bank of
windows. The train was arriving. He reached into his
pocket and offered the cat's eye again. Harry let it
fall into his palm. As it fell a great burden dropped
away too.

'Hurry. Hurry,' his father said.

Harry hugged his mother and father and gathered
his sack of apples and his belongings. He bounded
onto the train and took a window seat on the side
facing the station. He signed to his parents on the
platform. 'I write letter.' 'Will send more drawings,'
he said to Ray. 'Yes, same for you,' he said to his
sisters.

The train was pulling away. He climbed out of his
seat and raced to the windows farther back in the car.
His mother motioned, 'Good-luck. Good-luck,' and
shrank from sight.

Harry made his way somewhat unsteadily to his
place. He leaned his head back in the spacious seat

and rolled the marble between his fingers. He remembered his first journey to Mr. Bertie's school. He was so scared and lonely and angry. Not any more. He closed his eyes and gave in to the forward tug of the train. Whoa, the spell-down, his narrow escape, and his brave hearing friend — what stories he'd tell them at school.